MURDER Can Frost Your Doughnut

A HAUNTED CRAFT FAIR MYSTERY

Rose Pressey

www.kensingtonbooks.com

KENSINGTON BOOKS are published by

Kensington Publishing Corp.
119 West 40th Street
New York, NY 10018

All Kensington titles, imprints, and distributed lines are available at special quantity discounts for bulk purchases for sales promotion, premiums, fund-raising, educational, or institutional use.

Special book excerpts or customized printings can also be created to fit specific needs. For details, write or phone the office of the Kensington Sales Manager: Attn.: Sales Department. Kensington Publishing Corp., 119 West 40th Street, New York, NY 10018. Phone: 1-800-221-2647.

First Printing: October 2021
ISBN: 978-1-4967-3385-6

ISBN: 978-1-4967-3386-3 (ebook)

10 9 8 7 6 5 4 3 2 1

Printed in the United States of America

IF THE HAUNTING FITS, WEAR IT

"Cookie Chanel must investigate the horse-racing community to find a killer. . . . After *Haunted Is Always in Fashion*, Pressey's fifth amusing paranormal cozy is filled with quirky characters and fashion, along with a few ghosts. Fans of Juliet Blackwell's 'Witchcraft' mysteries may enjoy the vintage clothing references. Suggest also for fans of Tonya Kappes."

—***Library Journal***

"Haunted by three ghosts, a young woman searches for a jockey's murderer at the Kentucky Derby."

—**Kirkus Reviews**

HAUNT COUTURE AND GHOSTS GALORE

"It was a pleasure to read. I listened to this one, and I'm so glad I did. The novel is narrated by Tara Ochs. She does a fine job of narrating, keeping up the pace and differentiating voices well. The story moved right along. If you have a chance to listen, I recommend it with this one."

—**Jaquo.com** (on the audio edition)

FASHIONS FADE, HAUNTED IS ETERNAL

"Chock full of ghosts, supernatural guardians, cats possessed by spirits, a handsome police officer boyfriend, and tips on surviving the afterlife and vintage shopping."

—***Kirkus Reviews***

Books by Rose Pressey

The Haunted Craft Fair Mystery Series
Murder Can Mess Up Your Masterpiece
Murder Can Confuse Your Chihuahua
Murder Can Haunt Your Handiwork
Murder Can Frost Your Doughnut

The Haunted Vintage Mystery Series
If You've Got It, Haunt It
All Dressed Up and No Place to Haunt
Haunt Couture and Ghosts Galore
If the Haunting Fits, Wear It
Haunted Is Always in Fashion
A Passion for Haunted Fashion
Fashions Fade, Haunted Is Eternal

The Haunted Tour Guide Mystery Series
These Haunts Are Made for Walking
Walk on the Haunted Side
Haunt the Haunt, Walk the Walk
Walk This Way, Haunt This Way
Take a Haunted Walk with Me
Hauntin' After Midnight
Keep on Haunting
You'll Never Haunt Alone
The Walk That Haunts Me
Haunted Girl Walking
Walk in My Haunted Shoes
A Haunted Walk to Remember
Haunt with Me
Haunt Like Nobody's Watching

The Halloween LaVeau Series

Forever Charmed
Charmed Again
Third Time's a Charm
Charmed, I'm Sure
A Charmed Life
Charmed Ever After
Once Upon a Charmed Time
Charmed to Death
A Charmed Cauldron
Almost Charmed

Praise for Rose Pressey and her delightful mysteries

MURDER CAN CONFUSE YOUR CHIHUAHUA

"A North Carolina painter solves the murder of a fellow vendor at a craft fair with the help of her trusty Chihuahua and a ghost she's reincarnated through a painting."

—Kirkus Reviews

MURDER CAN MESS UP YOUR MASTERPIECE

"Plucky, self-employed heroine, cute pet, scary ghost, and two eligible suitors: everything a cozy needs."

—Kirkus Reviews

"The paranormal twist adds a bit of flair to this quirky new series."

—The Parkersburg News & Sentinel

"Rose Pressey's books are fun!"

—*New York Times* best-selling author Janet Evanovich

IF YOU'VE GOT IT, HAUNT IT

"A delightful protagonist, intriguing twists, and a fashionista ghost combine in a hauntingly fun tale. Definitely haute couture."

—*New York Times* best-selling author Carolyn Hart

"If you're a fan of vintage clothing and quirky ghosts, Rose Pressey's *If You've Got It, Haunt It* will ignite your passion for fashion and pique your otherworldly interest. Wind Song, the enigmatic cat, adds another charming layer to the mystery."

—*New York Times* best-selling author Denise Swanson

"*If You've Got It, Haunt It* is a stylish mystery full of vintage fashions and modern flair, with a dash of Rose Pressey's trademark paranormal wit for that final touch of panache. Chic and quirky heroine Cookie Chanel and a supporting cast of small-town Southern characters are sure to charm lovers of high fashion and murderous hi-jinks alike."

—*New York Times* and *USA Today* best-selling author Jennie Bentley

"Absolutely delightful! Prolific author Rose Pressey has penned a delightful mystery full of Southern charm, vintage fashion tips, a ghostly presence, and a puzzler of a mystery. With snappy dialogue and well-drawn characters in a lovely small-town setting, this thoroughly engaging story has it all."

—*New York Times* best-selling author Jenn McKinlay

"Fun, fast-paced, and fashionable, *If You've Got It, Haunt It* is the first in Rose Pressey's appealing new mystery series featuring clever vintage-clothing expert Cookie Chanel. A charming Southern setting, an intriguing murder, a stylish ghost, a tarot-reading cat, and a truly delectable detective combine to make Ms. Pressey's new Haunted Vintage series a sheer delight."

—*New York Times* best-selling author Kate Carlisle

"Prolific mystery author Pressey launches a cozy alternative to Terri Garey's 'Nicki Styx' series with an appealing protagonist who is as sweet as a Southern accent. The designer name-dropping and shopping tips from Cookie add allure for shopaholics."

—Library Journal

To my father. He always came to my rescue when I needed him. He was my real-life superhero. I love and miss you, Dad.

Chapter 1

Travel Trailer Tip # 1
While staying in your trailer, you'll want to explore your new surroundings. Taking a walk to check out the scenery is a fantastic activity. Just make sure to be on the lookout for suspicious characters.

The last rays of sunset faded and the sky turned a deep navy blue as evening arrived at the Sevier County Fair. A late summer breeze ruffled the leaves of nearby oak trees. Lights dazzled on the Ferris wheel and carousel, waiting for the nighttime riders. Carnies yelled as my best friend Samantha Sutton and I strolled by the ring toss game.

"Five tries for a dollar. Come on, pretty lady, give it a whirl," the sweaty man with a blond mohawk called out.

I ignored his request.

Soon he turned his attention to the person walking behind me. "Come on, big guy, I know you want to win a prize for your girl."

Memories of attending the fair with my parents flooded back. That had been twenty-some years ago. My father always won me a stuffed animal. He was the best at shooting the little ducks with the water gun. I missed those simpler times.

Not that they wouldn't be here tonight. Soon my parents and brothers would arrive. That meant Samantha and I would only have a short time until the chaos ensued. My father and brothers tended to be unknowingly mischievous. They were basically walking disasters. I had thought about attaching cautions signs to their backs in the past. As long as I kept them from the hazards around the fair, I figured things would work out all right. Though I suppose for them, all things were hazardous. They could injure themselves with a pillow.

Keeping them out of trouble was a full-time job. My mother knew that all too well. She'd been shepherding my dad and brothers out of potentially perilous situations for years. It was a wonder her hair hadn't fully turned gray. She still had dark hair like me. I described the shade as a night sky with touches of walnut mixed in. Those were two of my favorite paint colors I liked to use. Everyone commented on how we could be twins. Just like me at a little over five foot tall, she packed a powerful punch.

The smell of deep fryers and manure drifted through the air. An odd mix for sure, and not appetizing at all, yet that hadn't stopped people from indulging in the deep-fried butter and deep-fried candy bars. The hum of the machinery from the nearby Tilt-A-Whirl made it difficult to hear my best friend as she posed a question to me.

"What?" I asked.

"Is it just me or could that man be Johnny Cash's twin?" Sammie asked louder this time as the man walked by us.

Samantha, or Sammie as everyone called her, was the opposite of me in the appearance department. She was tall with blond hair the shade of a glass of bubbling champagne. In the past six months she'd grown out her locks a bit, but it was still styled in a bouncy bob.

"Oh, it's not just you. He is almost the spitting image of Johnny Cash, all right. He's here for the celebrity impersonation contest." I turned my attention to a red balloon that floated skyward.

Someone would be upset that they'd lost it. With so much activity, taking in every detail of this current setting proved difficult. Being an artist meant I liked to study my surroundings. It came in handy when I wanted to paint from memory. Plus, it was useful when being questioned by the police. Trouble seemed to follow me lately. I hoped that was all behind me. The police part, of course, not the painting.

"Really? Who else is here? Maybe I can get some autographs." Sammie wiggled her eyebrows.

"All the iconic country stars. Johnny Cash, Patsy Cline, Loretta Lynn, Dolly Parton, and even Elvis Presley." I ticked off the list on my fingers.

"Oh, Elvis? You know I love Elvis." Sammie fanned herself.

"Who doesn't love him?"

"You mean young Elvis or older Elvis?" she asked.

"Both," I said with a smile.

"Even better. I love both," she said. "So, there's like a big contest for the impersonators?"

"Yes, it's held at the end of the fair, but they have other shows leading up to that. One of them is tonight, I think."

"Okay, I'm on the hunt for an Elvis." Sammie scanned the crowd.

The county fair was in full swing. Not only were there rides and games and plenty of bad food to eat, there was an arts and crafts section too. I had set up a booth, hoping to sell some of my paintings.

Last year I'd become a full-time artist, and although it had been rocky at times, I felt as if things were going well. I had no idea becoming an artist could have such an . . . interesting start. I learned that, apparently, I had some kind of psychic ability that channeled through my art. Ghosts tended to appear when I unknowingly painted them.

I painted truly mystifying images and then the spirits came through the paintings. At first, I hadn't believed my eyes. I thought maybe I had lost my mind. But once I spoke with the ghosts, there was no denying it. Even my best friend Sammie had seen the spirits. Not to mention a few other people too. At least I knew it wasn't just me witnessing the insanity.

Sammie had been reluctant to come with me to the fair at first. She said all the food was too tempting and she hated dealing with the mosquitoes. But I'd convinced her to make the trip and poke around the midway before the arts and crafts fair section opened tomorrow.

Somehow, I'd also talked her into getting a candy apple and just watching as others took a spin on some of the rides. I'd told her maybe I'd ride the Ferris wheel, but I wasn't much for thrill seeking. I liked to play it safe. People would say that wasn't true based on some of the things I got into sometimes. But like I said, trouble seems to find me. I don't go out searching for it. I had ghosts telling me that they could help me solve murders, so the way I saw things, it was my duty to investigate the crimes.

Sammie wasn't the only one with me tonight. In my arms was Van. Or, if we were to call him by his full name, Vincent Van Gogh. My tiny white Chihuahua had been my sidekick since I'd discovered him at the shelter. When our eyes met, it had been love at first sight. We'd been inseparable ever since. He'd gotten his name because of his one floppy ear. It seemed like an appropriate moniker.

Sometimes Van liked to walk on his leash, but currently I held him in my arms because he'd gotten tired from all the excitement. Plus, he loved being snuggled up next to me. I enjoyed the cuddling just as much. We were like two peas in a pod. I suspected he'd perk up when we neared the corn dog vendor.

"Oh, check it out. There are the candy apples." Sammie pointed. "I can't believe I let you talk me into this."

"I want caramel with nuts." I sounded like a kid again.

Sammie and I approached the stand that sold the apples, cotton candy, and pretzels. It would be hard to walk away with just one. The junk food aroma wafted through the air, making my stomach rumble to attention.

I'd just paid for my apple when Sammie said, "Don't look, but your family's here."

"What?" I said. "They weren't supposed to be here until tomorrow."

"I guess they changed their mind," she said with a grimace.

I loved my family dearly, but if trouble followed me, then double trouble followed them. Chaos trailed along with them like a tornado swirling across the sky, destroying everything in its path.

"Have they seen us yet?" I asked, trying to hide behind a tall, bald-headed man next to me in line.

The man pinched his eyebrows together and moved up a couple of steps.

"Oh, you know you're not going to be able to hide from them," Sammie said. "Plus, yes, they've seen us. They're practically running over here. Bless their hearts."

I turned around and made eye contact with my mother. She gave a half-hearted wave, as if to apologize. My brother Stevie accidentally knocked over the trash can as he lumbered toward me. Hank waved frantically. They were carbon copies of my dad. Average height, but solidly built. Their dark hair hadn't grayed like my father's yet, but if they kept up their frantic pace, it probably wouldn't be long. Either that or they'd turn my hair gray from the pure stress of it all.

My brothers saw nothing in front of them because they only ever focused on one thing at a time. At the moment, that one thing was me. They resembled babies learning to walk for the first time as they bounded toward me. Sammie and I gaped at my family, unable to take our eyes off them. I was waiting for something else disastrous to happen.

"Only one trash can down. Not too bad," Sammie said, taking a bite of her apple.

"Let's step away from the food stand in case they crash into it," I said.

"Good thinking," Sammie said around a laugh.

Sammie and I walked toward them. Van trotted along beside me on his leash. When they neared us, my dad smiled, but then headed toward the food stand like a bloodhound sniffing out a clue. My mother didn't get a chance to speak a word because she hurried after him.

"Eddie, where do you think you're going?" she yelled. "No, you don't need a corn dog. You just had food."

No doubt he'd end up getting the corn dog anyway, and probably a couple of other things in the process. I suppose just this once tonight would be okay as long as he was good on his healthy eating plan the rest of the week. My mom had her hands full between watching after my dad and my brothers.

"How's it going, Sis?" my brother Stevie asked.

"Just checking out the fair, guys. What are y'all doing here? I thought you were coming tomorrow. And you've been staying out of trouble, I hope. Not destroying anything?"

That was more of a plea than a question.

"Hey, what does that mean?" Hank raised an eyebrow. "You're always thinking the worst, aren't you? Don't be so negative."

"What's up, Sammie?" Stevie wiggled his eyebrows.

When she smiled, Hank winked at her and Stevie shoved him. They'd always had a thing for Sammie. I'd cautioned her not to get involved with dating either one of those two. Not that they weren't sweet, but I wasn't sure Sammie was the best match for either one.

"We're here for the celebrity impersonation show. Mom and Dad want to see it," Stevie said.

"When does it start?" I asked, licking the caramel from my lips.

Nuts that had once been stuck to the caramel dropped onto my white tank top. Some fell toward the ground, landing on my brown cowboy boots. I'd worn my denim shorts too. Sammie said my outfit was perfect for a night at the fair. I was used to having paint stains on my clothes, but not sticky sweet candy toppings.

"In about five minutes. Are you going?" Stevie asked, though his attention was focused on Sammie.

After brushing the crumbs from my shirt, I turned to Sammie. "What do you say? Should we watch the show with this bunch?"

She finished her apple and then said, "Sure, why not."

"Who performs first?" I asked.

Stevie shrugged his muscular shoulders. "I don't know for sure, maybe Patsy Cline. There's a big Elvis grand finale."

"Oh, I'm eager to see Elvis," I said excitedly.

"Who isn't?" Sammie said, practically swooning.

"You like Elvis, Sammie? I do a good Elvis impersonation." Stevie swayed his hips.

I groaned. "Please don't ever do that again."

Stevie and Hank gestured at a couple of people they knew.

"I have to hand it to them. Your brothers like to have a good time." Sammie tossed the core and stick into a nearby trash can.

"Don't remind me," I said around a sigh.

After my mother and father joined us, we headed toward the stage to watch the show. My dad, of course, had a giant corn dog with mustard slathered over it. Not only had he gotten the corn dog, but he'd managed to finagle the jumbo-sized one they had been advertising on the poster in front of the concession stand.

"I see Dad won the battle," I said as my mother walked beside me.

Van wiggled in my arms as my mom scratched behind his ears.

"I told him that's the only one for today," she said.

"Only one corn dog or only one treat?"

"That one corn dog is the only treat he's getting, of course," she said without confidence.

I knew he wouldn't pay attention to her. My father had diabetes and other health issues, so my mother was always after him to watch what he ate. Tonight, she would have a battle on her hands. There was just too much temptation.

I was torn between wanting him to be happy, getting what he wanted, and wanting him to be healthy and stick around with us longer. I didn't want to lose him. My heart melted when I saw how happy my father was as he walked along with his family, enjoying his corn dog. I suppose I was a lot like him. Everyone said I was just like my mother. Of course, we had the same dark hair and eyes, but I had a lot of my father's traits too. Without a doubt, I also had my quirky moments.

My family and I gathered in front of the stage. A large banner announced the Fifth Annual Music Legends Tribute Contest. My brothers fought over who stood next to Sammie. Ultimately, they figured out one could stand on either side of her. Speakers flanked the front area of the stage with multicolored spotlights shining toward where the performers would stand. Other lights shone out into the crowd. The sky had turned completely dark, with a million stars twinkling in the black expanse. The temperature was perfect for the event at a pleasant seventy degrees. A microphone was in the middle of the stage, waiting for a performer to take the stage.

People were crammed together waiting for the action to start as a warm, gentle breeze carried across the wind. Even with these perfect conditions, a sense of uneasiness fell over me. What was wrong? Why did I feel so antsy? The evening had been flawless so far. I had to shake off the feeling. Nothing would bother me as soon as the show started. At least that was what I tried to tell myself. So why wasn't it working? Why did the feeling remain?

At the corner of the stage, I saw a shadowy figure moving away from the area. The thing that caught my attention first was the person's outline against the nearby canvas tent flap. I couldn't quite make out what the person was doing, but something about their actions seemed suspicious to me. Call it intuition, I suppose. It seemed as if the person was sneaking around, specifically trying not to be caught. And perhaps hiding something close to his body, so that no one would notice. Why would he do that? Was that a white jumpsuit the person wore? With bell-bottoms and an oversize collar?

CHAPTER 2

Travel Trailer Tip #2
Stargazing on a warm summer night is another fun activity. As always, when gazing upward, you should also watch for anything suspicious about your surroundings.

I contemplated walking over there to see what he was doing, but I reminded myself to stay out of trouble. Sometimes my inquisitiveness got me mixed up in a few snafus. My brothers called it nosiness. What did they know anyway? Whatever this person was doing was none of my business, I reminded myself. He was probably just setting up equipment for tonight's performance.

Nevertheless, I watched the area for several more seconds for any sign that the man had returned, but he had most definitely disappeared. No need to worry, I told myself. The strange feeling I sensed was probably just jitters from worrying about the craft show tomorrow. I turned my attention back to the stage. After all, no one else had noticed or acted as if the person's behavior was anything out of the ordinary.

Band members filed onto the stage and picked up their instruments. Bright lights illuminated the stage. As I swatted at the mosquitoes buzzing my head, I wished I'd brought insect repellent.

Finally—Patsy Cline stepped onto the stage. Well, not the real Patsy, of course, but an impressive look-alike. Her long, gold, sequined gown sparkled under the stage lights. She opened her mouth and her melodic voice flowed out. My mom and dad held hands as they swayed to the music. The Patsy impersonator sang one of my favorite songs, "Why Can't He Be You."

Sammie poked me in the side and then pointed toward the backstage area. "It's Elvis."

I only caught a glimpse, but just the sight of the impersonator made me swoon a bit. His dark hair and gold suit let me know this was the 1957 Elvis. Which song would he sing first? "(Let Me Be Your) Teddy Bear"? "Don't Be Cruel"? It was impossible for me to pick my favorite Elvis song. I loved them all.

"There's a Johnny Cash over there." Stevie pointed toward the man dressed in black at the corner of the stage.

We enjoyed several more songs from Patsy, and while she sang "Sweet Dreams (of You)," I scanned the surroundings again, checking for any sign of the suspicious character from before. *Nothing to worry about, Celeste. Stop seeking out bad stuff.*

Elvis wasn't due to hit the stage for another twenty minutes, so I decided to take Van to my trailer. He was probably hungry and wanted a nap. I would hurry over to my trailer and be back before Elvis uttered the first word of "All Shook Up."

I touched my mother's shoulder to get her attention. "I'm taking Van back to the trailer for his nap, Mom. I'll be back in a few minutes."

"Just be careful, dear."

My mother always instructed me to be careful no matter if I was going two steps away or cross-country. It was just her thing, I guess. Another one of her quirks. We all had them. Though a disconcerting feeling had settled in my stomach. Why did I have to obsess about completely innocent things?

Pushing the thought out of my head, I marched out across the green lawn toward my pink Shasta trailer. It was my home away from home during a craft fair. I rolled up to each venue with my pink-and-white truck towing the tiny trailer. Both were my pride and joy. Word had gotten out around town about my art. It was kind of hard for me to go unnoticed with my pink mobile art studio. Everyone remembered me. With any luck, that would bring in more buyers for my paintings. However, sometimes being remembered could be a bad thing.

The fairgrounds made such a lovely setting for the arts and craft fair. During the day, the nearby wildflowers added bursts of color, but the dark of night concealed the blooms. A pale crescent moon slipped in and out of view through the trees. Music and cheers drifted across the wind. Then, I heard a rustling noise from my left. Van barked and we turned our attention toward the nearby wooded area. A chill ran down my spine. The secluded area provided plenty of places for danger to lurk. Perhaps a wild animal?

"Hello?" I called.

No one replied. Did I expect a possum or skunk to answer me? Again, I was being too paranoid. With no other sounds, I continued toward my destination. I'd already parked my truck and trailer at the spot where I'd set up my booth for the next three days. With everything mostly ready for the festivities starting tomorrow, I only needed to set up my canvases in the morning.

Other vendors had set up their booths for the sale, with most of them putting up tables and signage tonight in preparation for the event. Probably so they could sleep in just a bit longer in the morning. Art vendors weren't the only ones with trailers around. Some of the other fair staff had places to stay around here too. The head of the art fair had told me some of the celebrity impersonators had trailers here as well. Maybe I'd run into some of them. My mother would love it if I snapped pictures of a few Elvis impersonators.

Coincidentally, after I walked just a short distance more, I spotted an Elvis impersonator coming out of a trailer up ahead. He stopped at the door and peered around, as if he was trying to see if anyone watched him. His strange behavior made me hesitate. Not wanting him to see me, I moved over to a nearby oak tree, hoping I hadn't already been spotted.

With Van in my arms, I hid behind the trunk, peeking around the edge. The smell of a nearby honeysuckle bush drifted through the night air. Unfortunately, I was too far away to get a glimpse of the man's face. All I saw was his white, bejeweled jumpsuit and dark hair. Was he wearing a wig? After a few more seconds of scanning the surroundings, the Elvis impersonator hurried away from the trailer. Stepping out from behind the tree, I was almost certain he hadn't seen me.

"That was strange, Van," I said.

Van barked as if he knew exactly what I'd said. The Elvis impersonator walked out of sight. As I neared the trailer the Elvis impersonator had stepped out from, the creepy feeling clung to me like lint on Johnny Cash's black pants. Right away, I saw the trailer's door was slightly ajar. Maybe the wind had blown it open? Was this the Elvis impersonator's temporary residence? Van's ears perked up and he growled, sending me a warning. Something about this scene just wasn't right.

Inching closer, I nudged the door open with my foot. After recent events, I'd learned not to mess with a crime scene. The hinges groaned with the movement. I placed Van down on the ground and held his leash. Surprisingly, he didn't bark as he walked with me up the trailer steps. It was as if he knew this was one time when his alerts weren't needed. My heart thumped wildly when I spotted the man on the floor. He didn't move.

The closer I got, the more I realized the severity of the situation. A man dressed in a gold jumpsuit lay on the trailer floor. Was he alive? I used my phone to shine light on the scene. The man showed no signs of life. With a wire wrapped around his neck, he was still clutching a doughnut in his right hand.

CHAPTER 3

Travel Trailer Tip #3
If you have company in your trailer and want to play a game, consider playing cards or a board game. Hide-and-seek might be a bit of a challenge.

My legs shook and my hands trembled. Did I have the nerve to check the man for a pulse? I had to do it. What if he was still alive? Another Elvis impersonator had just left this one's trailer, so that had to be the person responsible for this horrible act, right? No more wasting time. I had to help him. This Elvis impersonator's life might depend on it.

"Hello? Sir, are you okay?" My voice wavered as it broke the deadly silence.

Of course, he didn't make a sound, and I hadn't expected him to answer. What a silly question. A wire was wrapped around his neck. Clearly, he was far from okay. Dark cloaked my view of the entire scene, but I thought his face had turned a pale shade of blue.

What had I been thinking in coming in here? More like I hadn't been thinking. I suppose I wasn't quite sure how to react. Panic always made me do strange things.

Stop messing around and check on the poor man. I needed to check for a pulse. No more delaying. If he was alive, I would call for an ambulance.

"Hello," I called out again. "Are you okay?"

That seemed like the right thing to say before I entered his personal space. Kneeling beside the body, I placed my fingers against his wrist. No pulse.

I swallowed harshly, my eyes traveling to the glazed doughnut that was still clutched in his hand. Van eyed it and sniffed from afar.

"Don't even think about it, Van," I warned.

The detectives would not be happy with me contaminating a crime scene by allowing my dog to eat some of the evidence. I had many questions about the treat in question. Like would this man seriously still have a doughnut in his hand while being strangled? It had to be staged. Someone was making a statement by placing that doughnut in his hand. But what did it mean?

Suddenly, a thought crossed my mind. Was I putting myself in danger being here? What if the killer came back? No, that wouldn't make sense. Why would he risk returning to the scene? It wasn't like he'd come back to the trailer for the doughnut.

A rustling noise captured my attention. Maybe I was wrong—maybe the killer *had* returned. Why had I come inside this trailer?

"Hello," I called out. "Is someone else here?"

It was silly to ask, as if the killer would really announce his presence, but I was panicking. I needed to run out of there as quickly as possible. Hearing a noise while standing next to a dead body wasn't a good thing, yet it was as if my legs were frozen. Van hadn't barked, which gave me some relief. If someone else was truly around, I counted on Van to warn me.

I glanced over my shoulder to see if someone was standing behind me at the door. Thank goodness no one was there. Not that I could see, at least. The trailer was dark, the only glow coming from the tiny light on my phone. Rushing away from the body, I pushed my legs forward and ran for the door.

As I raced away, I glanced behind me a few times to see if anyone else was around. By all appearances, it seemed as if I was the only one in the area. Where had that Elvis impersonator gone? What did he know about the dead man on the floor? The police would want to talk with him right away. But how would they find him? How many Elvis impersonators were here at the fair? What if someone had just dressed like Elvis as a disguise and they weren't part of the county fair's act at all?

I replayed the scene in my head. Had there been anything that stood out to me that would lead me to the killer? I supposed I needed to slow down a bit. I didn't even know the victim's name yet and I was already trying to solve the crime.

Music boomed across the night air. No one had a clue what had happened just a short distance away from the stage. A killer was out there somewhere in the crowd, concealed by the dark and the activity around him. Maybe he was even ready to get on the stage to perform. The thought sent a shiver down my spine. What would happen next? I suspected the police would want to speak with everyone dressed as Elvis. But first, I had to call to report the crime.

The murdered man had been dressed in a gold jumpsuit. His dark hair had been slicked back into the familiar pompadour. Was this the man I'd seen sneaking around the stage earlier? Had he seen his killer?

The scene flashed in my mind again. A cable had been wrapped tightly around his neck. It occurred to me then that it was almost certainly a microphone wire. The jelly doughnut in his hand had one bite taken out. He hadn't even gotten to eat his doughnut. The poor guy. How sad was that?

I scooped Van up. "We have to go for help."

My adrenaline ramped up as I ran like a gold medal Olympian from the scene, heading back toward the stage area. With a shaky hand, I pulled my phone from my pocket. I moved it through the air. Just my luck, there was no cell coverage. I couldn't get a call out. Was this really happening? I'd just have to keep trying until the call went through.

Trekking across the grassy area, a strange feeling came over me, as if someone watched me. When I glanced over toward a line of trees, I noticed an Elvis impersonator. The rhinestones on his costume sparkled under the moonlight. He leaned against one of the tall oak trees. Even though he was a good distance away, I knew he was watching me.

I tried to memorize his features, but he was so far away that it would be impossible to pick him out of a crowd. Especially a crowd of other Elvis impersonators. Most of them were all dressed in some variation of a white jumpsuit. I wouldn't be able to shake a stick without hitting an Elvis. They buzzed around the fairgrounds like a swarm of bees in a garden.

Quickly, I shifted my attention away from the man, hoping he wouldn't come after me. I picked up my pace, running toward the stage even faster. No matter how fast I tried to move, though, it felt as if this trip was taking forever. The distance to the concert area seemed twice as long, as if I were on a treadmill.

Finally, I made headway. I spotted my family and Sammie in the distance. I weaved around groups of people swaying to the music. Unfortunately, the cowboy boots I'd worn weren't exactly the right shoe choice for running away from a killer. I slipped on the wet grass and fell face forward. I managed to catch myself a bit with my hands, but I had grass stains on my shorts. Of course, that was the least of my problems.

I tried to climb up from the damp lawn, but I kept slipping. Van licked my face, wagged his tail, and then jumped on my back. He thought I was playing a game with him.

"No, Van, it's not playtime. We have to get out of here before something bad happens."

I scooped him up and hurried the rest of the way. As I grew closer to my family, Sammie spotted me. A frown spread across her face. She probably wondered why I had a freaked-out expression on my face. Not to mention that I was running full force toward her and had grass stains on my legs and shorts.

Just when I thought I might collapse from exhaustion, I reached my clan. It felt as if I had no air left in my lungs. Sammie was the only one paying attention to me. Everyone else watched the stage, engrossed by the performance, totally clueless, as usual.

"What's wrong?" Sammie asked.

I tried to catch my breath as she fanned me with her hand, her expression growing more confused by the second.

"There's been a murder." The words spewed from my mouth. "At least, I think there's been a murder. There's a man back there in a trailer who has a wire around his neck. I'm pretty sure he didn't do that to himself. And I think Elvis did. Well, another Elvis. Oh, and the dead guy has a half-eaten jelly doughnut in his hand!"

"Are you sick? What are you talking about?" Sammie asked as she pressed her hand to my forehead to see if I had a fever. "Have you been drinking? Did someone slip you moonshine? That stuff will grow hair on your chest, Celeste."

I grabbed her by the arm and stared into her big blue eyes. "Listen to me. I have not been drinking. There's a dead man in a trailer back there, and I'm pretty sure he was murdered. I think an Elvis impersonator might have killed the man inside. Who, by the way, happened to also be an Elvis impersonator."

I couldn't get any clearer than that. I hoped Sammie would believe me despite my rambling. Sammie had to have faith in me. She was my best friend. That was what best friends did. Accepted everything as the truth no matter how crazy, right?

"Oh my gosh." Sammie shook my arms, what I'd told her finally registering. "Do you know what this means?"

"What does this mean?" I asked with some confusion.

She gave me another shake. "It means there could be a killer anywhere in this crowd."

Sammie was freaking out more than I was. Usually,

she was calm, but the wild, wide-eyed gaze had me concerned. I hoped she didn't faint.

"Don't panic," I said. "We'll be fine. Everything will be fine."

"Wait. Did you say he had a jelly doughnut in his hand?" With a lift of her sculpted eyebrow, Sammie's expression changed on a dime.

CHAPTER 4

Travel Trailer Tip #4
Never try to play truth-or-dare with a ghost.
The ghost might be more daring than
you are!

Instead of panicked, she seemed perplexed. Almost amused. I hoped she didn't think I was playing a prank.

"Yes, a doughnut. I guess he was eating." I shrugged. "But maybe it was just staged to appear that way."

"That doesn't make much sense. What do we do?" Sammie asked.

"We just have to call the police," I said. "What we need to do is get out of here before we become the next victims. Maybe this person wants to kill all of us." A wild flare flashed in Sammie's eyes, as if someone had just pressed her panic button again.

"Okay, just calm down," I said, gesturing with my hands for her to take a deep breath. "If the killer wanted to kill anyone else, I'm pretty sure he would have done it."

"I'm not so sure about that, Celeste," Sammie yelled over the music.

A new song had started and, with it, an upgraded level of volume. The rhythmic beat thumped in time with my heart. Maybe Sammie was right. I was trying to calm myself, but my nerves got the better of me.

Nevertheless, I said, "Inhale and exhale, Sammie."

Sammie blew out the air from her lungs. "You're right. We need to stay calm."

"We need to call the police," I said. "My phone isn't getting a signal, though."

"We're trapped here with no way to get help," Sammie said.

"That's not staying calm."

Sammie rubbed her bare arms, as if fighting off a chill, her eyes darting about the crowd, as if expecting the killer to materialize before us. With the heat index, the temperature felt like a hundred and twenty, but it was probably really ninety-eight degrees. Sammie's tank top clung to her sweaty body. No doubt the chill she tried to fight off had come from spine-tingling fear. Van barked, as if completely agreeing with her uncertainty. She didn't need the encouragement.

"I'll see if your phone works." I pulled the phone from her hand.

"What's going on with you two?" Stevie asked, finally noticing that something was amiss.

I pointed in the distance toward the trailer, but I still couldn't fully convey the gravity of the situation in words.

"Celeste said something about a murder," Sammie said, speaking for me. "She's calling the police."

"A murder?" My mom snapped to attention.

"What about a murder?" Hank asked.

"An Elvis impersonator was murdered," I said as I moved the phone through the air. "Still no signal."

They stared at me as if I'd completely lost my mind. I wished this was just some wacky prank I'd conjured up, but sadly, that wasn't the case.

"She's lost her marbles again." Stevie whirled his index finger next to his temple.

"I know it sounds crazy, y'all, but it's the reality of the situation. I mean, could I really make something like that up?" I asked.

"Well . . ." Hank said.

"Shut up, Hank." I touched the phone's screen again, trying to get the call to go through.

Sure, I had a vivid imagination, but I wouldn't make up something like this. Why would I want to freak everyone out with a crazy story about murder? The phones still weren't picking up a signal. Why was no one's phone working? This left me with no other option. I'd have to get away from the area to see if I could find service. I didn't want to leave my family here either, just in case the killer really was still hanging around, but what other choice did I have?

"I'll be back in a bit. Don't move," I said as I took off.

"Where are you going?" Sammie yelled out.

There was no time to answer her question. As I booked it out of the crowd, I almost bumped into a tall, lanky redhaired teenager.

"Is your phone picking up a signal?" I asked, my voice tinged with a frantic energy.

He gaped at me as if I was nuttier than the nuts covering the candy apple in his hand. After a couple of seconds with no response from him, I moved on to find a different way to call.

A young blonde holding a large, pink cotton candy in one hand and a phone in the other was a few steps in front of me. She seemed friendly based on the smile on her face. Anyone who liked cotton candy had to be sweet, right? Plus, it appeared her phone was working because she was pointing it in the direction of the stage.

When I approached, I blurted out, "Is your phone working? I can't get a signal on mine."

She shook her head. "Nope. Phones aren't working out here. I was just snapping a photo."

I couldn't believe in this day and age we couldn't even get a phone to work. I considered sending a kindly worded complaint to AT&T. Someone grabbed me from behind and I screamed. When I spun around, I pulled my arm back and landed my fist into the person's stomach. Stevie held his abdomen and groaned. My entire family had disregarded my instructions and followed me across the grassy lawn to the edge of the concert area. We stood near a hot dog vendor. Van sniffed the scent of mustard and onions that drifted across the night air.

"What are you doing?" Hank asked. "Are you trying to kill Stevie?"

"No, what I'm trying to do is call the police." I waved my phone around the air frantically.

"That's it. There's no turning back for her. She's lost her marbles. Are you sure you saw a murdered guy?" Hank asked. "Maybe someone was just playing a prank?"

"That's impossible. I know what I saw," I said defensively.

He held up his hands. "Okay, I believe you."

"Punched by your sister. Just like old times," Hank said around a laugh.

"Dude, she punched you too," Stevie snapped.

My mom held up her hand, and instantly, my brothers stopped bickering. "Enough of you two. Tell us what happened, dear. And start at the beginning."

"There's no time to start at the beginning," I said. "I'll tell you after the police get here."

Unconcerned, my dad remained entranced by the Patsy Cline impersonator on the stage. Everything was business as usual for him. But that was his typical behavior. He tuned out pretty much everything around him. I wished I had that quality sometimes. When it came to stressful situations, I took after my mother.

After moving a bit farther away from the stage area, I finally picked up a couple of bars on the phone. With a shaky hand, I touched nine, one, and one on the screen. Before I had a chance to hit Send, everything changed.

Chapter 5

Travel Trailer Tip #5
If you decide to play twenty questions, don't forget to stop at twenty. Beyond that point things can get dicey.

A loud boom interrupted the music. Screams rang out as everyone ran for cover. Candy apples and cotton candy flew from hands near and far. A couple of men wearing white shirts with the word Security written across the front rushed the Patsy Cline look-alike off the stage. I ran with my family and Sammie to a nearby food stand.

We hunkered down, hoping there would be no other shots. The smell of hot dogs hung in the air. When I glanced over, I spotted my dad reaching for a relish-covered frankfurter. My mom yanked the food from his hand. Even in a life-or-death situation, she wouldn't let him break his diet.

"What's happening?" Sammie asked.

No one answered her. No one had an answer, I suppose. I prayed the chaos would be over soon and that everyone was safe. I peeked up from the counter and saw a few people still scattering away from the scene. Sirens sounded in the distance. It seemed Sammie had been right, and we should have run for cover a long time ago. We could have gotten farther away and clear of danger.

After pulling out my phone, I saw that it had signal bars at the top of the screen, indicating that it should work. I touched the screen and the call appeared as if it was going through. I suppose it didn't matter, though, because it sounded like help was on its way. Nevertheless, the authorities wouldn't know about the murdered man in the trailer.

Seconds later, a woman said, "911, what's your emergency?"

"Yes, ma'am, shots were fired at the county fairground and I found a dead body," I rushed the words out.

"Leave it to Celeste to still be polite when she's been shot at," Stevie remarked.

"Well, I taught her manners. You should remember that." My mother frowned at Stevie.

"You said you found a dead body?" the operator asked.

The sound of her typing in the background carried across the line. I felt somewhat relieved just to have gotten the words out.

"That's right. I found a body," I answered.

"You saw the active shooter?" she asked, with more of the ticking sound from the keyboard in the background.

"Saw him? No, I didn't actually see anyone with a weapon," I said.

I mean, I'd heard the shots, but I never saw an actual person with a gun.

"Officers will be there right away," she said in a calm voice.

How could she be so unruffled about this? I knew that things had turned into complete chaos. Within a couple of minutes, the cops would arrive, and even more candy apples would be ruined when they stormed the area.

The operator asked if the shooter was still here. There was no way I would peek around to find out. I supposed I hadn't been sure the noise we'd heard had been a gunshot. But after finding that body, I wasn't taking any chances. None of us had an idea of what the loud noise had been. Would Caleb or Pierce show up on the scene? After all, they were both law enforcement. I'd met them at my first craft fair. That seemed like ages ago. In reality, it hadn't been long at all. Both men knew of my strange skill of painting ghosts into this realm. Surprisingly, they hadn't labeled me bonkers either. For that, I was grateful.

If they showed up here, wouldn't they be surprised to find out there had been a murder? However, they wouldn't be shocked when they found out I'd been the one to find the body. Once again, I had attracted trouble. Questions whirled in my head again. Over and over in my mind. Was the killer the one responsible for the loud bang? Did he have a gun too? Probably so. There was just too much crazy stuff going on for me to process everything.

"Thank goodness the police are on the way," I said when I ended the call.

"I guess we won't get to see Elvis or Johnny?" Hank asked.

"They'll probably give us a rain check," Stevie said.

"I think the least of our worries is the show," I said, peeking out over the top of the food stand.

A few of the braver folks were easing out from their hiding spots. In my opinion it was probably better to wait until the police told us it was safe to come out, even if there had been no other sounds of gunfire.

"Just asking," Hank said defensively.

To my left, I spotted the police in their black uniforms. A SWAT team? Additional officers moved stealthily to my right. When I checked over my shoulder, I spotted more of them behind us.

"We're surrounded," I said.

"Don't make any sudden moves," my father said, finally acknowledging the situation.

When I glanced over to the left, I spotted Detective Pierce Meyer, with his cropped dark hair and his dashingly handsome features. I felt heat rush to my cheeks. His dark suit fit his muscles in all the right places. Under the jacket he wore a crisp white shirt and a blue tie. With the other officers dressed in SWAT team gear, he seemed a bit out of place.

Seeing him didn't surprise me. He knew I was here at the fairgrounds, so it was understandable he would hear the call and show up on the scene. Nor should he be shocked to see me in the middle of all this action.

I wished he had come down to the fair under better circumstances. I'd been surprised to find out that Pierce was a budding artist himself. Although Sammie said he was only doing it so he would have a reason to come around more often. Even if that were the case, I thought it was awfully sweet. Pierce remained somewhat of an enigma to me to this day. He was always kind and funny, but he had a mysterious air about him that I was unsure I'd ever penetrate.

Where was Caleb Ward, my other detective friend, though? I'd talked to him earlier in the day. He knew I was at the fair this weekend too. In fact, he had a booth here at the fair as well, though he hadn't arrived yet as far as I knew. He said he had police work and would have to set up his wood sculptures later. Would this event shut down the entire fair? It seemed likely, which made me sad.

Caleb was a sculptor, and a great one at that. That wasn't his full-time job, though. Like Pierce, Caleb was a police detective. Caleb and I had been what my Aunt Patsy called "an item" for a while, but it was nothing serious. Not that my mother or Aunt Patsy didn't want it to be meaningful. They wanted him to be my steady, my one and only. Though they were quite keen on Pierce too. What would I do with both these great guys in my life?

Aunt Patsy owned Paradise Café, a cozy restaurant that offered little in the way of healthy cuisine. However, if someone wanted dishes loaded with gobs of cheese and butter, Paradise Café was the spot. Caleb loved to go there for the delicious, juicy burgers. Aunt Patsy was all for me being his girlfriend, so I was pretty sure Caleb had been sneaking over there and talking to her. She wanted to convince me to be Caleb's one and only. I wondered if Pierce would find out about that and start frequenting Aunt Patsy's place too, to get her on his side.

Van wiggled in my arms, snapping me out of my musings and drawing my attention back to the more important and dangerous scene at hand. As Pierce ran across the midway with a couple of other officers behind him, I watched him, partially to see what played out next and also because his good looks always caught my attention. Pierce scanned the surroundings as if searching for someone. Had he noticed me watching him yet?

It wouldn't be easy to explain why I'd been in that

dead man's trailer. Pierce and Caleb always asked me why I put myself in danger. It wasn't as if I did it on purpose! Okay . . . sometimes I did it on purpose, but I was usually just trying to help.

A couple of seconds later, Pierce turned his attention to me. It was as if he'd switched on his Celeste detection radar. I contemplated ducking behind the food stand again. It was too late, though. He'd already seen me.

"Oh, it's Detective Pierce," my mother said with a wave, acting as if Pierce had stopped by her house for tea and cookies.

"That scowl on his face tells me that he's unhappy with you," Sammie said.

"Maybe he thinks Celeste was the shooter," Stevie said around a snort.

"Knock it off, guys," I said.

While the other officers surveyed the surroundings, Pierce headed toward me. With Van still cradled in my left arm, I half-heartedly waved with my other hand. Pierce stepped right up to the hot dog stand.

"Are you okay, Celeste?" he asked. "Is everyone all right?"

Well, at least he'd asked about my welfare before inquiring about why I was in the middle of all this. He probably had no idea I'd been the one to make the call.

"We're just fine," I said.

"Speak for yourself," Stevie said, rubbing his stomach.

"Do you know if it's safe?" I asked. "Is there a shooter?"

"As far as we can tell, it was just fireworks," Pierce said. "No shooter at all."

We all breathed an audible sigh of relief.

"Do you know anything about someone being murdered here at the fairgrounds?" Pierce studied my face.

Why did he assume I knew something about that?

"Yes, I do know something about a dead body here at the fairgrounds," I said.

I explained the whole scene, as crazy as it sounded, even down to the jelly doughnut in the dead guy's hand.

"I need you to take us to the trailer," Pierce said.

I was afraid he would say that. I didn't like the idea of going back. A shiver ran down my spine at the thought. However, I knew I had to do it. There was no telling how long it would take the authorities to locate the right trailer if I didn't point it out. Although they could just find the one with the door open, I supposed.

"Are you sure it's safe to walk around?" my mother asked.

"Yes, Mrs. Cabot. Like I said, it was just fireworks," he said.

"Okay, I'll take you to the trailer." I turned to my family. "I'll be back."

"Be careful, honey," my mother called.

"Are you sure this is safe, Celeste?" Sammie asked.

"She's with a cop. Of course she's safe," Stevie said.

When I handed Van to Sammie, he licked her face. "I'll be back soon. Watch Van for me, okay?"

I didn't want Van involved in any more of this craziness. He'd seen enough. Pierce and I walked away from the hot dog stand, leaving the blinking lights from the abandoned rides behind. A shooting star flashed across the black sky overhead. A thick, damp heat lay like a blanket over the fairgrounds.

With nervousness dancing in my stomach, I wasn't sure what to say to Pierce. We walked across the grassy area toward the trailers. I figured it was best if maybe I waited for him to talk first. He surely had a lot of questions.

A few seconds later, Pierce said, "I just can't understand why you thought it was a good idea to go into a trailer. Someone else's trailer."

"Something wasn't right," I said. "What if I could have saved that man?"

Pierce couldn't argue with that logic, right?

"What if the killer had still been there?" Pierce asked with a frown.

Okay, so he could argue with my logic. I should have known.

"You have a valid point and I appreciate you bringing that up," I said.

"Don't try to nice your way out of this, Celeste," he said. "I'm angry with you."

Chapter 6

Travel Trailer Tip #6
Sometimes traveling in your trailer can get stressful. Especially when you're being questioned by the police. Meditation can help you regain a sense of calm—after they've gone, of course.

Pierce was angry with me? I wasn't sure how to react to that. I thought I'd been doing him a favor. Next, he'd tell me not to get involved in the investigation. That would be like asking me not to paint. Or asking Van not to bark. It was unavoidable.

"Well, it's all said and done, so there's no need to be angry with me," I said.

"I doubt it's all said and done yet."

"What do you mean?" I asked.

"Until the killer is located, it's far from over. We have to make an arrest," Pierce said.

"Yes, I suppose you're right about that."

Pierce asked, "Why did you place the phone call saying there was an active shooter? Was it just because of the sounds? Or did you really see someone with a gun?"

The branches of the large oak trees swayed in the distance, causing the leaves to rustle. The eerie sound added to the already spooky situation. Crickets chirped in the dark, thick, wooded area behind us. I swatted at mosquitoes as they dive-bombed the exposed skin on my arms and legs.

"I technically never used those words, 'active shooter,'" I said. "I told her that there had been shots fired. How were we supposed to know it was someone celebrating the Fourth of July a little late? And no, I never saw anyone with a gun."

"Well, needless to say, there's been a crime. It will likely shut down the fair for a while."

"For the night? Or for the rest of the scheduled time?" I asked.

"Likely just for the evening. We'll have this area sealed off. Luckily, this section is closed off from the public."

"Meaning that the public isn't supposed to be back here. That doesn't mean that someone didn't come back here. I didn't expect to see you here. I thought you were working that stolen artwork case."

He glanced over at me. "I'm still working that case too. Tell me exactly what you saw, Celeste."

"I'm not sure what I saw," I said. "But I think an Elvis impersonator is potentially the killer."

"Elvis killed Elvis?" Pierce asked.

"That's the way it appeared to me. I mean, I saw him leave the trailer. He was acting shifty. That was right around the time of the murder, I assume."

"We'll get a time of death and be able to tell for certain."

"Maybe the man went to the trailer, saw the dead guy, got freaked out, and left," I said.

"That's probably not likely," Pierce said.

We'd reached the area for the trailers. Other officers and detectives followed as I led the way to the crime scene.

I stopped and pointed. "It's the blue-and-white one right there. But wait."

"What's wrong?" he asked.

"The door's closed. I didn't close the door. It was open when I first saw the trailer. Otherwise, I wouldn't have entered. And I left it open."

"And you're sure that's the one?" Pierce asked.

"I'm positive. There are no other blue-and-white trailers around here."

"Stay back here for a moment, okay?" Pierce gestured.

Pierce and a couple of other law enforcement eased up to the trailer with guns drawn. Should I take cover? I supposed they were being cautious, but the killer could have slipped back inside. Maybe that was why the door was closed. The officers opened it and as they edged inside, I held my breath. Seeing Pierce in action like this made me realize just how dangerous his job was. Maybe I saw why he was angry with me for entering the trailer.

My stomach tumbled with queasiness as I waited for Pierce to emerge from the trailer. After what seemed like an eternity, he stepped out of the tiny crime scene. A grim expression remained on his face. Pierce was fun to be around, but he wore a serious expression most of the time.

"Well? What happened?" I asked when he walked over.

"My guess is someone strangled him with the wire," Pierce said.

"Asphyxiation by strangulation. That's an intimate crime. You have to get up close and personal for that. I saw that on one of those shows on the crime channel."

"Stop watching those shows," Pierce said. "You don't need the encouragement."

"What are we doing?" I asked eagerly.

"Well, we'll remove the body and the coroner will give us a report. We'll get a time of death and go from there. Wait. Why am I telling you this?" he asked with a frown. "You're not involved in this investigation, Celeste."

I held up my hands. "Okay, I'm not involved in your investigation. I get that."

I wasn't involved in *his* investigation. But I would probe this on my own. Technically, I hadn't lied to him.

"You said there was a doughnut in his hand?" Pierce asked.

He wanted to ask me questions pertaining to the crime scene? I thought he wanted me to stay out of the investigation! Although smug, I didn't point that out. Because I might need him later on to answer questions for me, I'd go along with him.

"That's right. I'm sure there was a doughnut in his hand because I had to keep Van from eating it. I'm pretty sure it was jelly. Or blueberry perhaps? It looked kind of blue . . ."

Did it matter what flavor? Why was I babbling?

"The doughnut is gone, Celeste," Pierce said.

My eyes widened. "Who came back and got the doughnut? Don't tell me the killer came back to get the doughnut and ate it. That's gross."

"I don't know what happened. This is extremely odd." He raked his hand through his thick hair and stared off into the distance. "Could have been an animal, I guess."

I wished I could remember more about the man I'd seen leaving the trailer. Just one tiny detail that might reveal his identity. When I checked to the right, I saw nothing. I thought for sure I'd seen something white out of the corner of my eye. Almost as if it had been glowing. Someone dressed in white? It must have been my imagination.

Even more authorities had shown up—I supposed to take photos of the crime scene and search for any forensic evidence. The coroner would be here, probably at any moment. I watched as the police taped off the trailer with the dead man still inside.

"I guess if you're finished with me here, I should get back to my family. They're probably worried about me." I gestured over my shoulder.

"Well, I can understand why they worry about you," Pierce said.

Oh no. He was going to start telling me not to get involved again. I had to quickly change the subject. But what else was there to say? It would be awkward if I asked him if he wanted a candy apple or a cotton candy. Or if he was going to stop by the craft fair.

I held up my hand to stop him. "I know what you're going to say, Pierce. Again, I won't get involved in your investigation."

On the inside, I smiled at my tricky use of words. I said I wouldn't get involved in his investigation, but I'd sure launch my own. This was something I couldn't ignore. Curiosity about the killer's identity would burn inside me and the only way to extinguish that fire was to find the murderer.

"All right, but I'm going to hold you to that," he said, pointing his index finger.

"I assumed you would."

"Celeste, I appreciate that you're listening to me about leaving the investigating to the detectives, but before you go, I do have a few more questions for you."

"Like what?" I asked.

I thought for sure I had nothing else to say about what I'd seen in the trailer. What was left for me to add? I supposed because there was something nagging at the back of my mind. I just couldn't quite put my finger on it yet. Maybe if I concentrated more it would come to me. Maybe later, when I tried to fall asleep and all was quiet, it would come to me. Then again, it could cause nothing but a sleepless night, with no further insight into what I'd seen.

We'd be allowed to stay on the grounds because the crime scene had been secured. I wondered how close I could get to the scene again without receiving a warning from Pierce or Caleb. I just wanted another quick scan of the surroundings.

Pierce pulled a notepad and pen from his jacket pocket like some old-school detective, rather than using the iPhone I knew he had. I guessed he just liked to do it the old-fashioned way. Who was I to judge his detective skills?

"Okay, Celeste, start from the beginning," he said, with the pen poised over the paper.

"What?" I asked in shock. "I already told you everything. Why do you want me to start from the beginning?"

"Because I want to make sure you didn't leave out any details. Going over it one more time might spark a memory, and that's crucial at this very early stage of the investigation."

I wondered if maybe he was just trying to make me so sick of this investigation that I wouldn't want to be involved at all.

"Whenever you're ready," he continued.

He used a professional tone, sounding all businesslike. I preferred him the other way, when he was a bit flirtier, when he would offer a wink or a special little smile. Not that I would ever let Caleb know that.

I repeated everything I'd told Pierce moments earlier. If my mother was here, she'd say Pierce was only asking me to repeat myself so he could spend more time with me. I knew that wasn't the case. Pierce was too professional for that.

"Let me see if I have this straight. The Elvis impersonator left the trailer moments before you discovered the body. Then you saw the same Elvis again after you found the body and he was watching you." Pierce tapped the pen against the notepad.

"That's right. Wait, not exactly correct, I suppose. I don't know if it was the same person. I mean, there are a lot of Elvis impersonators around here." I gestured toward the stage.

In the distance, the empty stage served as an eerie reminder of the evening's horrible events. Lights still shone through the warm night, but the music had stopped. The only sound piercing through the dark came from the crackling of police radios, the chatter from detectives, and the murmur of the dwindling crowd in the distance.

When I glanced to the right, I spotted a man in the distance over by the big oak tree. The tall, dark-haired man watched us. Something seemed different about him, but I couldn't quite put my finger on it. I blinked, attempting to focus my eyes better. It almost appeared as if he was outlined in a white glow, almost like a halo around his entire body. It must have been a trick of the eye because the ring of radiance around him soon faded.

"Celeste? Did you hear me?" Pierce asked, snapping me back to attention.

"Sorry, I was watching that guy by the oak tree." When I focused again on the spot where the man had been standing, he was gone.

"What man?" Pierce asked.

"I saw a man over there." I pointed.

"Was it the Elvis impersonator?"

"I don't think so. This man was taller. It was far away, though, so I didn't get to scrutinize his face."

"But you're sure it wasn't the impersonator?" Pierce pressed.

"I'm positive."

"One second." Pierce motioned for me to stay put.

He stepped over to a couple of officers and they talked for a moment. I stared out toward the crowd in the distance. It really was time for me to get back to my family and Van. Though I couldn't just walk away from Pierce. I knew Van would want to get out of there. He'd been fidgeting before I left. But maybe that was because he enjoyed sniffing the fried-food-scented air.

A few seconds later, Pierce returned. "The officers will check the area to locate the man you saw."

"It was probably just a curious craft fair vendor," I said.

"One last thing, Celeste: Do you think you could give a sketch artist a description of the man you saw leaving the trailer?" Pierce asked.

"Well, I can try, but I think the sketch could easily be mistaken for any other Elvis impersonator," I said.

He couldn't help but chuckle. "Yes, I suppose you're right about that. You didn't get close enough to see any details?"

I wished I had better news for him. No matter how hard I tried to remember, nothing came to mind.

I shrugged. "I'm not sure, maybe."

"I guess it's worth a shot, right?" He winked, breaking the protocol.

"Yes, it's worth a try." I smiled, pleased by his familiar gesture.

Pierce released a deep breath and then shoved his notepad and pen back into his pocket. "All right, then, I suppose that's all the questions I have for tonight. I can arrange for the artist to stop by tonight."

"Great." I hoped I didn't sound too eager to get away from him. "But you know, I might be able to draw something for you."

"No offense, Celeste, but the sketch artist is trained on what questions to ask in order to get an accurate depiction."

"No offense taken," I said.

"Are you still staying here in the trailer tonight? You know I advise you not to do that."

"Why? Do you think the killer will find me?" I asked.

The worried stare I received in return answered that question for me.

CHAPTER 7

Travel Trailer Tip #7
Listen. Just listen to the sounds of nature. You may also overhear a conversation about a murder.

"But the police will be here, right? What harm can there be if I stay here tonight?"

Pierce frowned, and I figured he must know that Caleb would be at the fairgrounds tonight too. I'd told him last week that Caleb would have a booth here as well. Unless he was trying to forget.

"I'll walk you back down to your family," Pierce said.

He and I left the crime scene and headed back toward the food stands. As we left, the coroner passed by. I was glad I wouldn't be there to see the CSIs bring the body out. Discovering the man was bad enough. I wanted to put distance between myself and this crime scene for the moment.

"There you are," my mother said when she spotted us.

"We thought maybe someone had killed you, too," Hank said.

My mother swatted at him to get him to be quiet. I knew my safety had been the topic of their conversation. They'd probably had to restrain my mother so that she wouldn't come hunting for me.

"Everything's fine," I said. "Pierce just had a lot of questions for me."

"Why? Did you think my daughter had something to do with this crime?" My mother placed her hands on her hips.

"No, ma'am," Pierce said. "Just following procedure."

She cut through him with her stare. "Procedure my hind leg."

Uh-oh. Pierce might have inadvertently ruffled my mother's feathers. I needed to change the subject before this got out of hand. What if my mother threw a hissy fit? Would Pierce arrest her? When something involved her children, my mother was like an attack dog.

"Did they get that dead guy out of there yet?" Stevie asked matter-of-factly, moving the conversation along. "The body will start to stink soon."

Of course, I should have known Stevie would embarrass me in front of Pierce. My brothers had no filters on their mouths.

As my family bombarded Pierce with questions, I once again felt like someone was watching me. When I glanced over, I spotted Caleb, but he wasn't looking at me. That was odd. He was speaking with the police officers and not paying attention to me at all. It had felt like someone had been staring at me. If not him, then who? I surveyed all around but saw no one of note.

Caleb talked to another officer as they stood by the little cotton candy booth. Bags of pink and blue sweet, fluffy spun sugar hung from the ceiling of the booth, just waiting for the next customer. A few seconds later, Caleb must have sensed *my* stare because he turned his attention toward me. He was headed in my direction. Pierce hadn't noticed that Caleb was walking toward us.

Caleb wore khaki shorts, brown sandals, and a white Polo. In that outfit, he'd be mistaken for a fairgoer, not a detective. Though I supposed this was his night off, so I wouldn't have expected him to be dressed like a detective. He had a careless charm that drew people to him. Of course, I noticed the sexiness that oozed off him. He was a solid six foot tall and had a lean figure. He was an amazing specimen of masculinity.

"What's going on, Celeste?" Caleb asked as he neared.

Pierce whipped around when he heard Caleb's voice. Tension hung in the air, making it thick. It was like trying to breathe through pastel-colored cotton candy.

"I found a body in a trailer," I said, blurting out the words. Obviously, the stress was getting to me.

"It's like this guy has a Celeste radar," Stevie whispered loud enough for everyone to hear.

My mother poked him in the side. Stevie didn't even seem to notice.

"What happened?" Caleb ran his hand through his hair.

"I found a body in the trailer over there." I pointed.

"Why were you in the trailer?" Caleb asked. "It wasn't your trailer, right?"

"No, it wasn't my trailer," I confirmed.

Pierce stepped in and recounted the whole chain of events. At least I wouldn't have to tell the story again. Although I didn't need him to talk for me. He was just a little wound up. A murder investigation could do that to a person, I supposed.

"Psst," a male voice called out.

I whipped around to see if someone was trying to get my attention. Couldn't they see I was kind of busy? But I didn't see anyone watching me. Either the voice had carried across the summer wind from somewhere nearby or I was losing it. I turned my attention back to my law enforcement friends and family. It didn't seem as if Pierce and Caleb were friends at all.

Caleb eyed Pierce up and down. Pierce gave him the same penetrating stare. Did anyone else notice the thick tension in the air? The men were competitive with each other to say the least. It wasn't as if they were strangers, though. Quite the opposite. They'd known each other for quite a while. They'd even gone to school together. Someday I'd get one of them to open up about the rivalry and friction between them. Hopefully, it wasn't just me at the heart of it all.

Neither of the men seemed to like the idea of the other one talking to me. However, I liked both of them. I had no idea about their true feelings for me, but I assumed they both had interest in me romantically. Pierce seemed shyer about it, though. He hinted about dates instead of asking me for a specific event. However, Caleb let his feelings be known more by just coming right out and asking me to accompany him on a planned-out date.

But I wasn't going to tell one of them to get lost just because the other one wanted me to. That wouldn't be nice or fair. I wondered if I could ever get them on an actual friendship level. They had shown positive steps at times, but I still hadn't gotten them to the point where I'd like them to be. Tonight, though, something else seemed off, as if there was more going on than their usual manly rivalry.

"Detective Meyer, is it all right if I speak with you for a moment?" Caleb asked in a stern tone.

Apparently, this talk was official business. They both gave me the side-eye. Okay, I knew why Caleb wanted to speak with Pierce. They were going to talk about me privately. Pierce and Caleb would further discuss how I shouldn't have gone into the trailer and risked my life. It was already done, so why dwell on it?

After Pierce nodded in agreement, the men moved a few steps away, as if they thought I might be listening to the conversation. They spoke in hushed tones, so that I wouldn't be able to eavesdrop. Pierce and Caleb kept glancing over in my direction.

Because I knew they were talking about me, I waved. They didn't respond to my gesture and I assumed they were plotting on how to keep me away from this investigation. It wouldn't work, though. I had ways of getting to the bottom of things.

"What are they talking about?" Sammie asked.

Van wiggled in her arms. She placed him on the ground, handing me the leash. Van danced and pawed at my leg for me to hold him.

"I can practically read their lips," I said. "They're saying how Celeste's in danger if she tries to solve this murder. She's too snoopy for her own good." I picked up Van and held him in my arms.

"I doubt you need to read their lips to know they're saying that," Sammie said. "Oh, here they come."

"Well, at least they didn't fight each other," I said.

Sammie's eyes widened. "Have they done that in the past?"

"I think at some point, before I met them."

Pierce and Caleb avoided making eye contact with me as they walked over. One pretended to scan the surroundings to the left and the other did the same for the right side. They'd have to meet my stare at some point.

"Maybe I should get out of here before they talk to you," Sammie said as she rubbed Van's head.

"No way. I need you to help me out. If you're here, maybe they won't remind me that what I did was a bad thing."

"I can try," she said.

Standing in front of me, both detectives locked their stares on me like magnets. I suddenly felt a bit uncomfortable.

"I know y'all have something to say. You might as well just come out with it," I said.

Caleb crossed his arms in front of his chest. "Tell me again why you went into that trailer in the first place."

I thought I'd already answered that question.

I shrugged. "I just sensed that something was wrong and I went to check it out. That was when I saw the man on the floor."

"That's dangerous, Celeste," Caleb said.

"That's what I told her." My mother punctuated the sentence with a point of her finger.

"She doesn't listen," my dad added. "She's stubborn, like her mother."

I whipped around. When did he sneak up? He had a tendency to stealthily move around so that no one heard him. Surprisingly, my father's words were completely coherent this time. Usually, he talked so low that his words came out more mumbled, but not this time. He was loud and clear. I knew he wasn't happy with me. Apparently, no one was happy with me. At least Van seemed to tolerate me still.

"Who are you calling stubborn?" my mother asked, placing her hands on her hips.

We were getting completely sidetracked. Everyone had gathered around. Sammie watched me and my brothers shook their heads. They were all upset with me for going into that trailer.

A young blonde dressed in denim shorts and a pink tank top approached us. "Excuse me, are you the detective handling the murder?"

"I'm Detective Meyer," Pierce said, showing her his badge.

"I have information about the case," she said.

Aha. I wanted to hear what she had to say.

"Would you please step over here, ma'am, so that I can ask you some questions?" Pierce said.

The young blonde nodded and followed him a few steps away so they could talk privately. I wished I knew what she was saying. I knew Pierce wouldn't let me in on the details. There was no need for me to even ask.

"What's going on, Celeste? Are they going to arrest you?" Stevie asked, snapping me back to the current conversation.

"Of course they're not going to arrest her. I already told you that," my mother answered in frustration. "Right, Detective?"

She stared straight at Caleb, putting him on the spot to answer. I waited with bated breath for the response too.

What was taking him so long? Surely there were no grounds to take me into custody. Right?

"No, ma'am. They're not arresting Celeste," Caleb said. "And please, call me Caleb."

He had told her that before, but she liked to switch back and forth between using his first name and calling him "detective." It depended on how serious her mood was.

"Tell me everything you saw, Celeste," Caleb said.

How many times would I be asked to repeat this story? I was growing tired of the questions. There needed to be less talking and more searching for the killer.

"She's already filled me in on things," Pierce said from over Caleb's shoulder as he returned from speaking with the young woman.

Maybe I needed to get these two away from each other. What had the woman said to Pierce? The curiosity would get to me.

"She's already told you everything, but I'm asking for myself." Caleb didn't bother to glance back at Pierce. "I might not be directly on the case, but I'm still invested."

"I realize that, Detective Ward, but you're not on the investigation," Pierce answered with a bite to his words. "If I need your input, I'll let you know."

"I'm not trying to be on the investigation," Caleb responded with a snap to his tone.

"Okay, guys, I'm really tired." I gestured to call for a time-out. "It's been a long evening, so I was wondering if maybe we could wrap this up for the night."

At least their expressions softened when I posed this request.

"I think it's a good idea that we all get home," my

mother said as she grabbed my father by the arm and started to guide him away from the food stand. I thought she might frisk him on the way out to make sure he hadn't pocketed any of the fried food.

"Come on, Celeste," she called.

She also was under the impression I wouldn't stay here tonight, but I'd already made up my mind. I was still residing at the fairgrounds. They hadn't evacuated the place, so until they did, I was staying put.

CHAPTER 8

Travel Trailer Tip #8
Stay in touch with friends and family while you're camping in your trailer. You may need to call them for help—or give them an alibi.

"I'm staying here tonight," I said. "I'll call and let you know that everything's fine, though, so don't worry."

My mother spun around. Fury flared in her eyes. "You can't stay here with a killer around."

"Exactly," Sammie added.

I was surprised; I had figured she'd be on my side.

"It's probably best that you stay off the grounds for tonight," Pierce said.

"I concur," Caleb said.

My brothers nodded.

"What about everyone else here? They're not closing the fairgrounds, so why should I have to leave?" I asked defensively.

"She has a valid point," my father said.

What? I was actually shocked he'd said that. I assumed he agreed with everyone else.

"What are you saying, Eddie? You want your daughter in harm's way?" my mother asked with her hands on her hips.

"There's a police presence more than ever around here, so I feel like she'll be safe," my father said.

"Thank you, Papa." I squeezed him in a hug.

Was that the smell of icing on him? Did he have doughnuts hidden in his pocket again? If so, my mother would sniff those out soon enough. She had a nose like a bloodhound. Everyone remained silent as they eyed me. I supposed they knew he had a point, but would they admit it?

"Well, I suppose you've made up your mind and won't listen to a word I say. Just like your father." My mother tossed up her hands.

I knew she'd say that. They often accused me of being like each other.

"We'll walk you to your trailer," Pierce said, motioning toward Caleb.

I supposed Pierce knew he wouldn't be able to walk me alone. Caleb would insist on going too.

After I said goodbye to my family with hugs, Pierce and Caleb walked with me across the field headed toward my trailer. Van, wearing his white shirt with "I'm the Boss" written on the back, snuggled close to me as I held him in my arms. His body was relaxed and I knew he was ready for bed. Caleb was on my right and Pierce on my left. It was like having a police escort. At least no one seemed to notice that the police had me surrounded.

"I have to ask, Celeste, why were you by that Elvis impersonator's trailer?" Pierce asked.

"Well, I have to go past that trailer to get to my trailer," I said, as if it should have been obvious.

"Seems like going down that other path would have been faster," Pierce added as he pointed to the dirt path through the tree line.

"Yes, the trail over to the camp area at the south edge makes for easier access," Caleb added his two cents' worth.

I thought they were against each other, but now it seemed they were tag teaming against me. The detectives versus Celeste. I supposed when it came to the topic of my safety, they liked to work together.

"Well, that's not the path I took," I said.

"Did the man you saw say anything to you?" Caleb asked.

"He didn't notice me at first. If it hadn't been for the moonlight, he probably never would have seen me."

"And you probably wouldn't have seen him," Pierce said.

"That's probably true. We made eye contact when I saw him the second time. He was over by the trees. I think he knows I found the body. He has to be the killer."

"All right, so we're seeking an Elvis who killed another Elvis," Caleb said.

The lights of the Ferris wheel dazzled in the distance. "Exactly."

"You're sure you don't have any descriptions other than he's an Elvis impersonator? That's not exactly a lot to go on," Caleb said.

"Nothing else. There has to be some record of the impersonators who are here at the fair. You can find them, and you'll find the killer," I said with a wave of my hand.

"Let's hope it's as easy as that," Pierce said. "Unfortunately, it's never that easy."

"Unless you put a great detective on the case," Caleb said.

Oh no. The jabs were starting again between them.

"You don't really think the killer would come after me, do you?" I asked, feeling less confident.

"We won't think about bad things like that. Just focus on the fact that we'll find who did this right away." Caleb's calm voice carried across the night air like a gentle breeze.

"You won't have anything to worry about, okay?" Pierce reached over and squeezed my hand.

When Pierce touched me, a comforting feeling came over me. When I glanced over at Caleb, he was staring straight ahead. I had a feeling he'd seen Pierce touch my hand.

We continued around a small cluster of trees over to the spot I would be calling home for the next few days. I'd lucked out and had gotten a shady spot that had a beautiful view of the rest of the fairgrounds. Now that night had set in, the lights from the rides sparkled in the distance, not yet shut down, and the wind carried the faint scent of corn dogs and popcorn.

On the outside along the top of my trailer, I'd added twinkling lights that lit up the night. Well, my dad had added them and almost broken a leg doing it, but the lights were up there now and I loved them. However, because I'd failed to turn on those lights before leaving my trailer earlier, it was darker than I'd anticipated when we arrived.

"Well, here I am, guys. Thanks for walking me over." I tossed my hand up in a wave.

"Whoa, not so fast." Pierce held his hand up. "I need to check inside and around the perimeter to make sure it's all clear."

"I'll investigate inside while you secure the perimeter," Caleb said.

"I think it's best if I go inside," Pierce said with a stony glare.

The detectives stared at me as if I was the one who should make the call on who took which position.

"How about I go inside?" I asked. "You two can take care of out here."

When Pierce and Caleb laughed, I didn't even release a chuckle.

After a few more seconds, Caleb asked, "You're serious?"

"Yes, I'm serious. In the time you've been standing out here debating who should go in, the killer could have painted a reproduction of the *Mona Lisa*."

"Nevertheless, I'll check inside." Pierce stuck out his hand for the keys.

Caleb didn't debate any more as he walked around the side of the trailer and I handed Pierce the key to the door. After Pierce unlocked the trailer, he stepped inside, leaving me alone with Van. Weren't they worried about me standing outside with the potential killer around?

They'd failed to remember that I could be snatched away while they were checking the premises. I supposed I wouldn't point out that tiny flaw in their plan. I hoped the killer didn't actually show up, though. Crickets chirped in the nearby trees and a rustling noise caught my attention.

"Caleb? Is that you?" I whispered.

He didn't respond. Was it an animal? Perhaps a raccoon? Yes, that was probably it. Just a nocturnal animal scavenging for food. Nevertheless, I stepped closer to the trailer. At least I felt somewhat safer with my back pressed against the steel wall. Thank goodness a few seconds later Pierce emerged from my trailer. I mean, it was the size of a postage stamp, so I was surprised it had taken him more than two seconds to check things out.

"It's all clear in there," Pierce said as he walked down the two steps from my trailer.

I assumed it would be clear, considering I'd locked the door earlier when I'd left. No signs of forced entry either. I sounded more like a detective every day. I had to remember not to use those types of words in front of Caleb or Pierce . . . they might alert them to my plans.

"Thank you for checking," I said. It was sweet of him, even though unnecessary.

"Where's Caleb?" Pierce asked.

"Right here," Caleb said as he walked around from the side of the trailer. "No signs of anything suspicious."

"Okay, guys, it's been a long day. Time for Van and me to hit the sack." Van had already fallen asleep in my arms.

"Call me if you need anything. I'm just a short walk away," Caleb said.

"I'll be here if you need help," Pierce said. "I'll keep you updated. I don't want you to worry about this, okay?"

"Sure, I have faith in you."

Pierce was good at his job, and if at all possible, he'd nab the killer. Nevertheless, that didn't completely put me at ease. I knew there was always a possibility the killer would evade capture and possibly come after me. Especially if he thought I was a witness. Why had the man killed the other Elvis impersonator? More than ever, I felt I needed to check into this myself. The faster I found the killer, the better off I'd be.

"I certainly hope you are thorough with this investigation." Caleb turned to Pierce.

I walked into the trailer. As I closed the door, the detectives still watched me. I hoped they didn't bicker more now that I'd left them alone with each other.

CHAPTER 9

Travel Trailer Tip #9
Night walks can be relaxing. But not if there's a killer on the loose. Always be careful.

After putting out food and fresh water for Van, I placed him on his quilted bed. He circled around and found a snugly spot. My retro trailer was awesome, but when it came to space, I had to get creative. I'd learned early in my trailering adventures to bring only the essentials. My art supplies were crammed into a corner. Paints, canvases, and an easel. Luckily, my brothers had installed a metal-hitched storage area to the back of my trailer, allowing me to haul more of my paintings. Somehow, they'd paid attention and even painted the hitch the exact shade of pink that matched the trailer.

The trailer's benches and table that tucked into the back of the trailer converted into a bed. On top of the bed was the pink-and-white quilt my grandmother had made me. Along with toss pillows with patterns of pink hearts and gingham print.

I checked out the window, wanting to see if Pierce and Caleb had gone. There was no sign of the men. At least that was what I'd thought at first.

I spotted the silhouette of a man as he walked away from my trailer. The moonlight highlighted his form. That wasn't Pierce or Caleb. He seemed wider and shorter. Where had he come from? Suddenly, an abrupt snore erupted from Van. I turned to my pup and couldn't help but be momentarily distracted by his sweet face as he slept. By the time I looked at the window again, the man was gone.

With a gulp, I checked the locks on my door. Once I reassured myself that they were secure, I headed to my craft corner to retrieve a blank canvas and supplies. Time for work. The surge of urgency to paint came over me in waves, as if something nagged at the corners of my mind. I knew something or someone was trying to give me a message. There was only one way to get rid of this feeling. To paint. Maybe it would be another painting with a hidden image. Would that lead me to the killer? Of course, there was a chance none of this had to do with the killer, and the feeling I was experiencing was simply inspiration. There was only one way to find out.

After I placed the blank canvas on the easel, I gathered my paints. Sitting in front of the empty white backdrop, I closed my eyes and waited for an image to come to me. Visions flashed in my mind, like a blinking neon sign. With any luck, when I opened my eyes, I'd project that image right onto the blank canvas with my brush. It came so easily that it was almost like painting by numbers.

I grabbed my paintbrush, dipped it into the black paint, and then started making sweeping strokes on the white canvas. Stroke after stroke, using different brushes and assorted paints until soon the image took shape. I knew right away who this was. Anyone would know who this was right away. I felt giddy, like a teenager gushing over a crush.

Would a hidden image appear in this portrait? Would a ghost emerge from the canvas? Surely not. The ghost of Elvis? I wished! The best I could hope for was the message painted within the painting. I had to find it, even though it would be like hunting for a needle in a haystack. I really had to study the painting to see what was concealed within.

As I continued stroking the brush across the canvas, Van watched me as he sat by my feet, awake once more. He probably wished I had food instead of paint. He was like my own little vacuum cleaner, always nabbing the crumbs.

"I'll get you some treats soon, Van. First, I just need to finish up a few touches here and there, like the eyes and the gorgeous mouth."

The Elvis portrait had taken shape nicely. Yet, as I studied the canvas, I thought there was something a bit off about his appearance. Elvis was a hunk, a hunk of burning love. Actually, he might have been the most handsome man who ever walked the earth, in my opinion. I'd never seen him in person, of course—he'd died before I was born—but I didn't need to see him face-to-face to know.

I'd seen him in the movies and in photos, and that was enough for me to base my decision on. I could well imagine how magnificent he had been in person. However, this man on my canvas just didn't have that same je ne sais quoi. I thought maybe I was losing my touch.

"This man just doesn't look exactly like Elvis," I said, pointing at the canvas with my paintbrush.

Van barked, as if agreeing with me. My pup did that a lot. Not necessarily agreeing with me, but barking to voice his opinion. We didn't always agree. Like he thought he should get way more treats than I thought he needed. But I digress.

"It doesn't look exactly like Elvis because it's not Elvis," a male voice said from behind me.

Van barked wildly. When I screamed, I accidentally fell off the stool, tumbling onto the trailer floor. I peered up into the eyes of someone who looked an awful lot like Elvis.

CHAPTER 10

Travel Trailer Tip #10
Telling ghost stories can be the perfect campground activity. It's even better if a real ghost pops up.

Elvis was in my trailer.

Well, okay, a man who was clearly trying to mimic Elvis was in my trailer.

I scooted back on the floor, trying to put distance between us. Unfortunately, there was nowhere to go. The man stood near the door, so I couldn't run away from him. I was trapped.

"What do you want?" I asked.

Had he come to kill me? Was this the Elvis impersonator I'd seen leaving the crime scene? What would I do to protect myself? I had no weapons. Maybe I could use the easel to smack him over the head? Would Van bite the guy's ankle?

The man pointed. "You painted me. I should ask what you want."

What? I studied the man's face for a second. Was this really happening? This wasn't the killer? I studied his face again. It all made sense. He was a ghost. More specifically, the ghost of the Elvis impersonator I'd seen on the trailer floor with the wire wrapped around his neck and the jelly doughnut in his hand.

I wasn't sure what to say, although my mind kept thinking why couldn't this be the real Elvis? *Focus, Celeste, focus.* Nevertheless, I had to find out what this ghost wanted. Unfortunately, it wasn't that easy. Ghosts never knew why they came, and I never knew why I painted them. I had to assume this had something to do with his murder. He wanted me to find out who killed him.

"What's your name?" I asked.

No other questions came to mind. My voice sounded calm, though. I was acting like I was just chitchatting with a customer.

"Donald Moran," he said, tipping his upper lip to the side in Elvis style. "Nice to meet ya, ma'am."

"Nice to meet you too, um, Elvis . . . I mean, Donald." I climbed to my feet.

Did he want to be called Donald or Elvis?

"Either name is fine," he added, as if reading my mind.

I stayed back a bit, just in case this ghost wasn't nice. So far, he seemed fine, but things could change on a dime. Not all ghosts were friendly. Far from it, actually. The last thing I needed was a poltergeist in my trailer. Van remained quiet as he observed the ghost.

"Where are my manners? What's your name, gorgeous?" Donald stepped a bit closer.

That was far enough, Elvis.

I held up my hand. "No need to shake hands. I'm Celeste Cabot. Are you here about your murder?"

He scowled. "Murder? Why on earth would I be here for murder?"

Oh no. Did he not realize he was dead? How would I break the news? There was no easy way to give that kind of information. If he didn't remember what happened to him, he might ask how it had happened. I didn't want to tell him all the horrible details.

"It's just that ghosts come around because the person has been murdered or they have unfinished business and are trying to figure out why they're here. Do you have unfinished business?"

I thought maybe he'd take the hint with that question and realize he'd been murdered. The word "ghost" would hopefully clue him in.

"I don't think I have unfinished business," he said. "I died in a car accident, right? It was pretty straightforward as far as deaths go. It happens, unfortunately."

Oh dear. Either this was a different ghost or he was confused. At least he knew his living status, though. I studied his face, wondering if I was mistaken about his identity. Nope, that was definitely the man I'd found with the doughnut in his hand. Apparently, I would just have to come right out and tell him.

I cleared my throat. "Okay, here's the thing. I found you in your trailer. You were murdered. You didn't die in a car accident."

His gaze remained fixed on me as he stood there like a statue. "I don't believe you. You're wrong."

What could I do to convince him? My mind was blank on how to persuade him. Then I remembered the text exchange I'd had with Sammie about tonight's events. I grabbed my phone and scrolled to the words. It wasn't much, but it was better than nothing.

Next, I put the phone in front of his face. "Here, check it out for yourself."

"That doesn't prove I was the one murdered," he said with indignation.

"You're right, it doesn't prove that, but I bet tomorrow you will be in the newspaper. Oh wait. I bet they have a story online already. The media is fast, you know."

"This is ridiculous," he said.

I typed away and quickly found an article on the subject.

"Aha. Here you go." I showed him the phone again.

"Well, what do you I know. I finally made front-page news. Of course, I had to die to do it."

"Yeah, well, that's typically the way it works," I said.

"Wait a minute. That didn't list a name. Which means it doesn't prove that it was me."

"But it says so right here. I mean, it lists the fairgrounds and says an Elvis impersonator. That's pretty compelling evidence, don't you think?" I asked.

"Well, that's because you told them to write all that," he said.

He was just being difficult. Apparently, he was in denial too.

"Okay, what makes you say you died in a car accident?" I asked.

If he wanted to claim an accident as the reason for his death, he needed to provide details. Which I knew he wouldn't be able to do.

"I just remember it," he said with a shrug.

"Do you care to explain to me exactly what happened?" I asked.

"I could do that, I suppose, although it's terribly painful to recall the whole incident."

I hadn't thought about that. Maybe I shouldn't push him too hard. After all, it had only been a few hours since his death. There was no way this had been an accident, though. I hoped he soon realized that.

"Well, I suppose we could talk about something else," I said.

"I'm not sure what to say." Donald's blue eyes seemed brighter, as if he became even more vivid and real.

I supposed I could ask him to perform a few songs for me until he was ready to talk. I chuckled to myself. That wasn't very nice of me. I had to take this seriously.

"Well, if there was an accident, I guess there would be a police report. That would tell us exactly how you died," I said.

"I suppose," he said with a great deal of hesitancy.

"Great. Consider it done." I picked up the paintbrush to put the finishing touches on the ghost's portrait.

"How soon can you get that report?" he asked.

Considering Caleb and Pierce constantly told me not to get involved, I assumed they'd never want to give me a copy of anything relating to the murder investigation. And I knew there wouldn't be a police report of an accident. Once I showed Donald that there was no record of an accident, he would have to accept the reality.

"I could do it in the morning, I suppose."

"We can't put this off. I don't think that's fast enough," he said.

"I don't think I can get the information tonight," I said.

"Well, then, what else are we going to do?" The gold fabric of his suit made a crinkling noise when he moved his arm. Was that suit made of gold lamé?

“Do you have any suggestions?” I placed my hands on my hips.

“The night’s young. All this activity is right out the door.” He pointed.

I frowned. “I don’t like the sound of this. Plus, there is no activity. Everyone left for the evening when you were . . . well, they left.”

“You’re young. Go enjoy yourself.” He motioned with his hand. “Just because no one’s out there doesn’t mean you can’t enjoy the fair.”

“I’m tired,” I said around a forced yawn. “I don’t want to enjoy myself at this hour of the night.”

“I bet you’d wake up once you got out there and started having fun. Maybe have a shot of whiskey to wake you,” he added.

“No can do,” I said with a wave of my hand. “No drinking on the job. Plus, whiskey will put hair on your chest.”

“Well, you’re not a lot of fun, are you?” The corner of his lip lifted slightly as he asked.

“Hey, I’m a lot of fun. I painted you into this dimension, didn’t I?” I pointed at his portrait.

Could I paint him out? No offense to him, but he wasn’t a fun Elvis.

Donald released a boisterous laugh, scaring Van. Van raced over to me and hid behind my legs. Donald’s gaze shifted to Van. My puppy had been awfully quiet just watching the conversation until Donald scared him. Usually Van got protective if he thought someone might want to harm me. I suppose he felt no true ill will from the fake Elvis. Or should I call him Donald?

I picked up Van. “This is Vincent van Gogh, or Van for short.”

"Oh, I get it," Donald said with a chuckle. "The ear, right?"

"You got it," I said, rubbing Van's head. "He's my best friend."

"Well, you know my favorite mutt is a hound dog, but Chihuahuas are pretty good, too."

CHAPTER 11

Travel Trailer Tip #11
Explore your surroundings. You never know what evidence you might find.

Donald had mostly paid attention as I'd told him some of how I'd discovered his body. And that I'd seen an Elvis impersonator leave his trailer moments before I'd walked in to find him stretched out on the trailer floor. He'd intently listened to me recount the story, but the skeptical smirk on his face still said he wasn't convinced.

Furthermore, I wasn't sure how this had happened, but thirty minutes later, I found myself on the midway with the ghost. I'd changed out of my pajamas and into my tan shorts and blue tank top. The Elvis impersonator had stood outside my trailer door, waiting for me to change. I'd thought maybe he'd disappear, but when I stepped outside, he was right there, leaning against the Shasta.

I suppose Donald was way more persuasive than I ever thought possible because I had been determined to stay inside. Yet there I was, surrounded by the lingering smell of popcorn, cotton candy, and fried everything. Discarded food wrappers, ticket stubs, and half-eaten candy apples littered the ground.

"Fried doughnuts," Donald said with excitement as he pointed at the unlit sign.

"Oh, that's the last thing we need," I said. "Besides, they're closed."

Did I dare mention that he'd had a doughnut in his hand when I'd found him? Obviously, he had a thing for the sweet treats. I'd left out that detail, but I really was curious.

"Just because they're closed doesn't mean I can't fantasize about them," he said.

"Okay, you have me out here, what do you want me to do?" I asked.

Being out here alone on the deserted fairgrounds gave me a creepy feeling. Having a ghost with me didn't help either.

"Well, I think first off you should see if you recognize my killer." Donald adjusted the jacket of his gold suit.

After scanning the abandoned fairgrounds, I gazed at Donald blankly, flabbergasted that he'd asked this. "Are you serious?"

He scrunched his brows together. "Of course I'm serious."

The unwavering frown on his face let me know that he was 100 percent sincere.

"If you say I was murdered, well then, here's your chance to find the killer. What better way to track him down than to search for him here?"

"No one is here," I said, gesturing. "And even if we come back when the fair is in full swing, there will be a lot of people here and no guarantee that your killer would show up."

"Okay, maybe this isn't the best time, but you have to start somewhere," he said.

He was right. I had to start somewhere, but not here and not now. I wanted to find the killer. However, with the fairgrounds resembling a ghost town, tonight wasn't the time.

"Wait. Who was that?" Donald asked.

"Who was who?" I whispered.

Did I think someone would overhear us?

Donald pointed. "I thought I saw someone walk around that ride over there. Even more curious, he was wearing a white jumpsuit. I'm almost sure of it."

Was he pulling my leg?

"You just happened to see an Elvis impersonator, huh?" I scanned the surroundings for any sign of an Elvis impersonator.

But then I told myself that was ridiculous. Even if Donald had seen someone, more than likely the killer wouldn't still be dressed as an impersonator. The murderer would have changed clothing. Plus, I had no idea what the killer truly looked like. He could have blond hair, gray hair, or purple hair, for all I knew. That was because I was almost sure he'd been wearing a wig. Impersonators did that, right? Or did they? The more I thought about it, the more I realized some of them sported the Elvis haircut all the time. Donald's pompadour was all real. There was just no way to know if it had been a wig, I supposed.

"It's impossible to find a killer by just standing out here," I said. "No one is out here. Even if they were, I don't think I'd recognize them at all, not even an ounce of recognition."

"I guess you're right," Donald said, sounding defeated.

"Now that this excursion is over, we can go back to the trailer." I released another yawn.

"Not so fast," he said, pointing across the way. "I saw the Elvis impersonator again."

I tossed up my hands. "Oh, come on. You've got to be kidding me."

"A few men are standing over there." He motioned.

To my surprise, I spotted three men dressed as Elvis standing over by the bumper cars. I thought everyone had gone home for the evening. Where were the police? Why weren't they still here and questioning every single Elvis impersonator at the fairgrounds? Oh dear. If Caleb and Pierce knew I'd questioned their investigating, they wouldn't be happy with me. I wasn't questioning whether they were doing their jobs per se. I mean, I knew they couldn't patrol the grounds all the time. However, in my opinion, my question still seemed like a valid one.

One of the men seemed antsy. He kept scanning the area as if he was waiting for something or someone. Donald and I watched in silence as we hid behind the large pirate ship ride. A couple of minutes later, the group dispersed, but the antsy man remained. I knew that he'd been up to something. I supposed I needed to watch him to find out exactly what he was up to.

"What are you thinking about?" Donald asked.

"That Elvis impersonator over there is acting weird," I whispered.

"It's like you read my mind. We're on the same wavelength." He moved his hand back and forth, indicating that we were connected. "What do we do?"

"Well, we should move closer to that guy. If someone approaches him and they start talking, we'll want to hear what's said."

"I like the way you think," Donald said with a nod.

"I'm glad you approve," I said as I marched toward the man.

Thank goodness the stranger hadn't noticed us. At least not yet. Donald and I hid behind the pony ring. From this vantage point we had a clear view of the man. He still hadn't noticed that we were watching him. I hoped it stayed that way too. The man checked the time on his shiny gold watch.

"I suppose he's TCB," Donald said.

"TCB?" I asked.

"Taking care of business." Donald chuckled. "Get it?"

I studied Donald's face without speaking.

"Elvis used to say he was taking care of business," Donald explained.

"Oh, I get it. I got the joke." I grimaced at his lame attempt at humor.

"Tough crowd," Donald said with a click of his tongue.

Just when I was ready to give up watching the man, a young blond woman, probably around twenty-two years old, approached him. She wore denim shorts and a pink tank top. Then it hit me. This was the woman who had approached Pierce. What had she said and what was she doing now?

"Maybe that's his girlfriend," Donald said.

"Perhaps," I whispered.

Maybe this was nothing more than a guy waiting for

his date to show up. Although I suspected there might be something more serious about this guy based on his actions. I wondered how I could get Pierce to tell me what she'd said to him. Donald and I watched the couple. After a couple of seconds, the man checked his watch again. Aha. It was obvious to me that they were waiting on someone else. This wasn't a romantic interlude.

"This is strange," Donald said as he rubbed his chin in concentration.

"Yes, it is peculiar," I said. "I get a bad feeling about this little get-together."

Whoever was supposed to meet them must be late. Time ticked by with no sign of another person joining them. A couple of minutes later, the girl shook her head and then walked away. The guy remained, though. He must have decided to wait for the other person. I hoped we didn't have to hang around much longer to find out because I was getting tired. Though I supposed I'd watched for this long, so I wanted to stick it out.

"Wait. Here comes someone." Donald pointed. "That man's headed toward the bumper cars."

I spotted the tall, dark-haired man wearing a white shirt with the fair's logo.

"He works here," I said.

The fair employee stared right at the Elvis impersonator. Soon the employee stood beside the suspicious man. They talked for less than a minute before the men turned and headed across the midway. They'd never sensed me watching. No way would they have known a ghost watched them too.

"Well, what are you waiting on?" Donald asked. "We have to follow them."

"I don't know if that's such a good idea," I said, yawning. "It's late and their meeting probably has nothing to do with your murder."

"But you don't know that for sure." He gave me a pleading expression. "That is, of course, if I was truly murdered. Maybe you don't want to find out because you know I *wasn't* murdered."

"All right, I guess we'll follow them, but just for a little bit because, well, what if they're the killers? That could be dangerous for me." I eased away from the pony ring like a cat burglar.

How did I get myself into these situations? I needed to learn how to say no. Oh, who was I kidding? Snoopiness was in my DNA. As much a part of me as my dark hair and big brown eyes. I wanted to find out if the men had anything to do with the murder. I was using Donald as my reason for doing this, but I would've done it with or without him.

CHAPTER 12

Travel Trailer Tip #12
If you venture away from your trailer, make sure you remember where you parked it. You don't want to wander back to someone else's trailer by mistake.

Sneaking away from the rides and games, Donald and I trailed the men to the nearby field that adjoined the fairgrounds. Were the men actually leaving the area? I didn't have my truck keys with me, so there was no way I could follow them out of here. Donald and I would trail them as far as we could, but if they got into a car, the trail would grow cold. Maybe I could find out what type and possibly get the license plate of their vehicle, but other than that, my hands were a bit tied.

"Do you think they'll leave?" Donald asked.

I sensed his nervousness. He might have been a ghost, but his emotions came off strong.

"We'll just have to get as much info about them as

possible. Maybe we can get close enough so we can hear what they're saying," I said, trying to sound encouraging.

The men stopped in a parking area and stood beside a black Mustang. Were they waiting for someone else again? Donald and I hid behind a large oak tree. Well, I hid and he stood beside me. Being a ghost and all, he didn't have much need for hiding.

"We need to get closer," I said out of the corner of my mouth.

"We could slip behind one of those other parked cars." Donald pointed.

I scanned our surroundings for the best path to the parked car beside them. I had to stay under the radar. What was I thinking? They wouldn't know I was watching them, right? Or, then again, maybe they would. The Elvis impersonator could be the man who had watched me step out of Donald's trailer. Therefore, he might recognize me. Nevertheless, the only course of action I had was to casually walk across the area and act as if I had no idea the men were even around.

Donald strolled along beside me as I made my way to the red Ford Fusion that would serve as my hiding spot. I tried to act casual, as if I wasn't spying on the men. I just hoped they didn't notice me—no doubt I'd act completely obvious, like a deer with its eyes caught in headlights. If I wanted to be successful at this sleuthing, I needed to improve my snooping skills.

Once I was only a few steps away from my planned hiding spot, I ran over to the red Ford. I ducked down and inched my way around the car to the trunk, waddling like an actual duck. I peeked out over the taillight. The men remained in the same spot, and luckily, their conversation was loud and clear.

Donald knelt behind me as if anyone would actually see him. Nevertheless, I didn't point that fact out. Navigating the spirit world would take getting used to before he could become an expert. I was almost sure I wouldn't be able to steer my way through the ghostly world as well as he.

"Good deal. We'll talk soon," the fair employee said and then walked away.

"You have got to be kidding me." I tossed up my hands, having a stronger reaction than I'd intended. "As soon as I get here so I can hear, the guy walks away?"

"That appears to be the case, yes," Donald said.

The potential killer didn't leave, though. He leaned against the car and pulled out a cigarette. He lit it and took a drag. The woman he'd spoken with earlier walked toward him.

"Oh, maybe this wasn't a wasted trip after all," I whispered.

"You have to keep the faith," Donald said.

The blonde walked up to him and then leaned against the car next to him. For several seconds they didn't speak. The man offered her a puff of the cigarette. She waved it away.

A couple of seconds later, the Elvis impersonator asked, "Have the police talked to you?"

"Yeah, Justin, they've talked to me," the woman said with a ton of irritation in her words.

My eyes widened and I glanced back at Donald. Maybe we were on to something. I had the man's first name. That was definitely a step in the right direction.

"I didn't know what to tell them."

"Just don't say anything," he snapped.

Was he admitting that he was the killer? Was that why he didn't want her to speak with the police?

"It's hard not to say anything at all. They're putting pressure on me to talk." She glanced back and I ducked down again.

Maybe she'd sensed someone watching. My heart thumped faster again. And I'd just gotten it to settle down. I was going to need a cardiologist when all this was done. The last thing I needed was to be caught hiding behind this car. I just had to stay down here behind the fender and not peek out at them.

The impersonator then said, "How can you talk when you don't know anything?"

"What's that supposed to mean, Justin Blackburn?" she asked.

The fact that she had used his last name spoke volumes about her level of anger with him.

"You don't know anything about a murder." Fury filled his words.

Murder. The word reeked of guilt as it slipped from his lips. It seemed as if he was quite agitated with this woman. I wondered who she was. His girlfriend? Just a friend? Were they related? Maybe I needed to speak with her alone. She might be more willing to talk with me if she thought I wasn't with the police department. Sure, she might not want to confide in a total stranger, but perhaps I could befriend her. Okay, that sounded a tad devious. But if it meant trapping the bad guy, I supposed it was worth it.

"Just don't mess this up," he said. "I made it this far and I'm not going back to prison."

Donald gasped. Good thing they couldn't hear him. Okay, now I knew Justin had been in the slammer. What for? Murder? What would Caleb and Pierce say about this? How would I explain how I'd gotten this information?

"I'm not going to mess this up." The tremble in her voice made it sound as if she might cry.

"If you're the reason I go back . . ." His voice was threatening, like an animal trap just waiting to clamp its jaws on the unsuspecting prey.

She didn't respond as a long pause settled between them. Of course, this allowed my mind time to think of all the worst-case scenarios. I imagined she thought the same. What would he do to her? Kill her?

"Well, let's just say it won't be good for you," he added.

Their conversation stopped. What were they doing? Was he trying to hurt her? I peeked up from behind the car. The woman had walked away. He stood there for a bit longer, then headed in the opposite direction. What would I do? I couldn't allow this to end there. Going after him would be pointless, but I intended to follow her.

"What are we doing?" Donald asked.

"I can't let her get away. I need to follow her," I said.

She'd taken off walking across the parking area. I'd pursue her until I couldn't follow anymore. If she got into a car, well, that was where my trail would drop off like a boulder over a cliff. I dashed out from behind the car. The Elvis impersonator had headed back toward the midway, so he wouldn't see me. I ran fast, desperate to catch up to her.

"Okay, what's the plan, Celeste?" Donald asked excitedly.

He didn't know me well, but in the past few hours, I figured he would've caught a glimpse of the way I rolled. It was enough time with me for him to realize I was a fly-by-the-seat-of-my-pants kind of gal.

"There are no plans, Donald. We're just going to wing it." A surge of adrenaline coursed through me.

I thought I heard an audible gulp from him, which was interesting, considering he was a ghost. Nevertheless, I didn't have the time to dissect the logistics of ghosts and their bodily functions.

The woman walked at a brisk pace, making it hard for me to catch up. My petite legs provided a short stride. At least I was getting my cardio exercise for the day.

"Why is she walking so fast?" I asked.

"I guess she's in a hurry," Donald said.

"Well, I figured that much, but I want to know why," I said.

She walked toward a green pickup truck that was parked at the edge of the parking area. Actually, the truck was parked in the grass next to a sign that read No Parking. Obviously, she wasn't one to follow the rules.

The moon provided the only light. Darkness concealed my surroundings, making it impossible to see everything as it truly was. What color green was her truck? Chartreuse or lime? What was the make and model? How would I find her once she left this parking lot? And then she slipped behind the wheel of the truck.

"This is where we stop," I said, disappointment saturating my words.

"Too bad. I really thought we would get to talk to her," Donald said.

I was ready to give up . . . but then she turned her attention to me.

When our eyes met, I froze. This was my chance. I had to get her to talk to me before she took off. But what would I say? What kind of excuse would I give? I waved, and she reluctantly waved back, acting as if she was trying to figure out whether she knew me.

That was my solution. That was how I'd talk to her. I'd pretend I knew her. After that, I had no idea what would happen. Another bit of improvisation on my part. How would I segue the conversation into questions about a murder? That seemed almost impossible.

As I approached the woman, I noticed the scowl on her face. The moonlight shone over her blond hair and pretty face.

"Stephanie? Is that you?" I asked.

She eyed me as I moved closer. I hoped she didn't think I was a crazy person ready to attack her in a dark, secluded area.

"My name isn't Stephanie," she said suspiciously.

Maybe she could see right through my act already.

"Oh, I'm sorry, I thought you were my friend Stephanie," I said with a chuckle.

"Nope, not me," she said as she closed the truck door.

"Uh-oh," Donald said. "This isn't going well."

I didn't need him to point that out. I was fully aware that this plan wasn't going as I'd hoped. I had seconds to turn this around before she got behind the wheel of the truck and took off.

"Sorry about that." I turned to walk away, then stopped. "By the way, I love your truck. What color is that? It's hard to see in the dark."

I might not be able to continue the conversation, but I'd know the color of her truck. If she took off, I'd have something more to go on to locate her again. I thought my shift in this conversation had definitely moved in the right direction. But until she spoke again, I had no way to know for sure.

After a couple of seconds, she said, "They call it green mist metallic."

"It's unique," I said. "I love trucks. My name's Celeste, by the way."

"Easy does it, Celeste. You're dangerously close to creepy stalker vibe," Donald offered.

I supposed his observation was accurate. I didn't want to come on too strong.

"Thanks," she said. "I'm Kaye."

Her tone was still hesitant, but at least she hadn't told me to get lost. She'd given no last name, but Kaye was better than nothing.

"Nice to meet you. Do you work at the fair?"

She eyed me up and down. "No. My boyfriend is with the entertainment here."

"Well, we already knew that," Donald said. "But do continue."

He talked as if she was hearing his every word.

"I'm one of the arts and crafts vendors," I said.

She yawned, making it clear she couldn't care less. I had to move this conversation along.

"It's terrible what happened here tonight." After I spoke, I waited, watching her face for a reaction.

"Yes, it is tragic," she said, uneasiness in her voice.

I continued, "I wonder who would have done such a thing? Did you know the man who was murdered?"

"Why would I know him?" she snapped.

"Oh no, Celeste. What have you done?" Donald said. "You could have asked me if I knew her."

Wow, I hadn't expected such a sharp reaction from her or Donald. I had to fix this right away.

"Oh, it's just that you said your boyfriend was with the entertainment, and I heard the person who was killed was as well."

"Okay, good one," Donald said. "I think that worked. Nice save."

She studied my face for a moment. "Yes, I guess I knew him a bit."

"That's funny because I don't know her," he said.

"Do you have any idea who would have wanted to do this to him? I mean, should we all be afraid? Do you think we're in danger?"

"How am I supposed to know?" she asked. "I'm not the cops."

"Yes, well, are you scared about walking around out here at night?"

She shrugged. "Are you?"

"A little bit, yes," I said.

My uneasiness grew the longer I talked. If she knew her boyfriend was the killer, she might not be afraid to walk around out here at night alone. It seemed like I wasn't going to get her to divulge any info.

"I really need to get going." She gestured over her shoulder.

"Yeah, okay, I'll see you around," I said.

She climbed behind the wheel of the truck and drove off.

"I think she knows more than she wants to admit," Donald said.

"I think you're right."

"What will you do?" Donald asked.

"I plan on getting her to talk. I don't know how exactly, but some way, somehow, I will."

CHAPTER 13

Travel Trailer Tip #13
It's important to bring things along in your trailer that relax you. If you have a hobby, pack necessities for that hobby. Every amateur sleuth should bring a magnifying glass, flashlight, camera phone, and snacks.

Donald had stopped mentioning the car accident. It seemed as if he was fully on board with the fact that he had been murdered. I didn't push the issue, though. When he was ready to discuss his demise, he would. Back in my trailer, I examined his painting. Where would I go from there?

"Talk to me, Celeste. What's on your mind?" Donald asked.

Van pawed at my leg and I picked him up. "Hmm, let me think."

"I hope that doesn't take too long."

"Oh, I know!" My words came out with a touch too much enthusiasm.

"Oh, you scared me!" Donald had flinched and was clutching his chest. "You know what?"

"I'll check the painting and see if there's a hidden message." I pointed.

"You've confused me again, little lady."

"There are hidden messages when I view my paintings through a glass." I placed Van on the floor.

"That's certainly an interesting talent," he said.

"You have no idea." I picked up a jar and stood in front of the painting.

"That's an odd way of scrutinizing me by putting me in one of your paintings," he said with a nervous chuckle.

Things must be bad when even a ghost thought I was bonkers. No matter, this was my reality. With the jar up to my right eye and keeping my left eye shut, I scanned the portrait. I moved over the top of his head, the dark hair, and then down to the forehead. Next I arrived at the piercing blue eyes. Still nothing jumped out at me. No pun intended. His full lips, complete with the curled upper lip. Moving on, I trailed down the white, rhinestone-covered jumpsuit. My optimism was wearing thin.

After a couple of minutes with no luck, I was almost ready to give up. Yes, it had only been a couple of minutes, but it didn't take long to check the whole painting. Just as I'd hoped, an image was hidden within the picture. It wasn't visible to the naked eye, but the skeleton was painted into the Elvis jumpsuit.

The skeleton depicted in the image appeared to be dancing. I wasn't sure what this clue meant, but I knew there had to be some meaning behind it and it was up to me to figure it out.

I placed the jar on the table beside the easel and turned my attention back to Donald.

"What did you find?" he asked.

I explained the image to him, and that I had no idea what it meant.

"I wish I could hold the jar and see for myself," he said.

I felt bad that he couldn't see it. Maybe it was time for a shift in the conversation.

"Why don't you tell me a little about yourself," I said.

"I'm originally from Toledo," he said. "I was supposed to be married right before the accident."

"That's tragic," I said, feeling even worse for the man. "Is your fiancée here at the fair?"

"No, she's not here. We had a fight."

My interest piqued now. "A fight about what?"

He shrugged. "She thought I was flirting with the Patsy Cline impersonator."

"The same one who's at this fair?" I asked.

He pointed. "That's the one."

"Well, were you?"

"Of course not. I'm faithful," he said.

"Why are you here in Tennessee?"

"I travel all around for these gigs," he said.

"Kind of like me and my art," I said. "Did you talk to all the Elvis impersonators here at the fair?"

"I can't remember," he said with a frown. "As I far as I can recall, I've had no interactions with other impersonators."

All right, so asking him about conversations he'd had with other impersonators was out the window.

"I'll keep thinking about this. Don't worry, I'll figure it out," I said. "But in the meantime, I should hit the sack."

He gaped at me, as if he had no idea what I meant. He didn't think I'd stay awake all night, did he?

I motioned over my shoulder, hoping he'd take a hint and disappear back into the next dimension. Maybe he'd come back in the morning.

"I can take a hint. I'll be back tomorrow," he said with a tilt of his lip.

And with that, he was gone. I stood there for a moment and stared at the spot where he'd stood, hoping he wouldn't have any trouble returning. Neither one of us was well versed in the mechanics of ghostly travel, after all. But never mind that—it was a problem for the morning.

After changing into my pink pajama shorts with the Chihuahua print and a matching pink shirt, I put away the supplies and moved over to the little window. I peeked out the blinds. I wasn't sure why, but a strange feeling overcame me. I worried that something else might happen soon. The thought sent a shiver down my spine.

Trying to shake off the feeling, I climbed under the covers and closed my eyes. Van snuggled up next to my body. Thoughts of the murder filled my mind. Not exactly pleasant ideas to help me fall asleep.

But my exhaustion won out in the end because the next thing I knew, I was opening my eyes as sunlight streamed into the trailer. I blinked a few times, glancing around to see if my Elvis impersonator ghost had returned. There was no sign of Donald around.

Van hopped up from under the blanket, obviously ready for breakfast. A new day meant a new start. I had high hopes for it. With any luck, I'd get to the bottom of the murder investigation and I could wrap it up into a neat little package, tied up with a pretty pink bow.

I yawned and stretched as I got out of bed. Where would I start with my search today? I had to check the clue from the portrait again. But first, I had to fill Van's dishes. After I made sure my pup was fed, I went to the painting. Standing in front of it, I studied the image. Had Donald really been here last night or had that been a dream? I picked up the jar and checked the painting. The skeleton was still there. That much hadn't been a dream. What did it mean?

When a knock came at the door, I almost dropped the jar. Who could that be this early? Van barked, letting the person on the other side of the door know that he was ready to attack if needed. I was still wearing my pajamas. My hair must be a mess too. I tried to smooth down my flyaway strands and adjusted my pajama shirt so that it wasn't twisted on my body. When I peeked out the window, no one was there.

Chapter 14

Travel Trailer Tip #14
Bird-watching is another enjoyable endeavor. It's also a good excuse to spot more than just birds.

No other knocks sounded at my door. Though no one had been there when I checked, I was almost positive someone had knocked. After a quick breakfast of a protein bar, I dressed in my khaki shorts, pale yellow tank top, and white flip-flops. The forecast predicted another scorcher today. I left Van inside with the air conditioning on while I set out my paintings for today's craft fair. Well, actually, my first task wasn't to set out the paintings. I had something else planned.

When I stepped out of my trailer, a male voice called out to me. "What's happening, good-looking?"

I spun around to see Donald standing at the edge of my trailer. The ghost of the Elvis impersonator had returned. I'd started to think he might stay away for good.

I clutched my chest. "Oh, you scared me."

"Sorry to do that to you, darling," he said.

"Not a problem. It's just that with a killer on the loose, I'm a bit on edge. You understand, right?"

"One hundred percent I understand," he said as he moved closer to me. "I hope you forgive me."

"You're forgiven."

"Where are you headed to this morning?" he asked.

"Just on a little bit of a mission, I guess," I said as I headed away from my trailer.

Carnival music from the rides already filled the air. Blue sky stretched as far as the eye could see. Beams of sunlight bathed the area in a golden glow. Suddenly a late summer breeze ruffled the leaves on the trees behind me. I glanced back, struck by the thought that it might not be the wind at all. Not spotting anything in the trees, I shook my head and continued forward.

Donald fell into step beside me. "Where to?"

"I guess you could say I'm searching for the killer."

His eyes widened. "You're not going to confront the killer if you find him, right? Why would you do that?"

"Because I have to find the killer before he kills me."

"You really think the killer is after you?" he asked.

"Absolutely. I found the murder victim and I think he wants to find me. I'm a loose end."

"I've had time to think about this, and well, maybe that's a job for the police," he said.

"I'm just giving a little bit of extra help. This is my life we're talking about."

"I can understand that, but it seems dangerous," he said.

"I don't think it's any more dangerous than doing nothing," I said.

"Well, you're lucky you have this big hunk of love to come along and help you." He wiggled his hips.

"Do you always do that?" I asked with a frown.

"Do what?" He scowled.

"Try to act like you think Elvis acted?"

"Well, I *am* an Elvis impersonator."

"But . . ." I cut myself off before saying too much.

"But what?" he pressed.

"It's just that you're doing a really bad job of it." I grimaced, instantly regretting that I'd been honest with him.

"What do you mean?" The tilt of his lip had turned upside down into a frown.

"I just mean I don't think Elvis really talked like that. Maybe you'd better just stick to the singing. You do that well, right?"

I hadn't heard him sing, so I had no way to know.

"I used to think so, but I'm not so sure," he said.

He shuffled along beside me, as if he'd just been deflated. Oh no. I had upset him. I hadn't meant to do that.

"I didn't mean to hurt your feelings," I said.

"I'll be fine," he said with a wave of his hand.

Well, I felt bad. I'd have to make it up to him. If I'd been able to, I would have hugged him.

As I neared Caleb's trailer, I spotted him standing in front of the door. I really regretted that I hadn't applied makeup. Though I supposed he had seen me at some of my worst times. Like when being chased by a killer.

"Good morning," he said with a lopsided smile

"Good morning," I said, sounding a bit bashful.

He still made me blush.

"What brings you by here so early?" Caleb asked.

Oh no. He thought I'd come by specifically to see him.

"I guess I was just taking a walk."

My answer was vague, and I knew he picked up on that.

"I know you're busy, but would you like to get breakfast before the event starts? That is, unless you have other plans already." Caleb studied my face. "Actually, don't tell me," he said, holding up his hand. "You planned on going around this morning, trying to find clues."

"Oh, he's good," Donald said.

"Am I right, Detective?" Caleb asked.

I felt the heat rush to my cheeks. He knew me better than I'd realized. "Well, it's imperative that we act quickly," I said.

"And that's what the police are doing. You don't trust us to do the job?"

"I saw someone outside my trailer last night," I blurted out. I wanted to let him know that this was an urgent situation, for me in particular.

"You didn't tell me about that," Donald said.

"What did the person do? Can you give a description?" Caleb asked.

"I thought I saw the Elvis impersonator, and I thought maybe he was watching my trailer."

"What time was this?" Caleb asked.

"Probably around midnight."

"Maybe we should discuss this further over breakfast," he said. "Besides, you need your energy to find clues."

"This guy must really be hungry, Celeste. Go to breakfast with him," Donald said.

I smiled at Caleb. "Yes, I guess you're right about that."

"Do you want to meet me there or should we drive together?" Caleb asked.

"I'm not exactly dressed for going into a restaurant," I said.

He eyed me up and down. "It's just Patsy's place."

"I'm sure she'd be thrilled to hear you say that," I said with a chuckle.

"You know what I mean. She doesn't have a dress code for you."

"Oh, so you're saying that if she did, this outfit wouldn't make the cut?" I asked, teasing him.

"Quit while you're ahead, guy," Donald said. "Don't answer that question."

"You're gorgeous no matter what you wear." Caleb winked.

Butterflies swarmed in my stomach. I was a sucker for compliments.

"Nice save," Donald said.

"We can drive together if you'd like," I said. "I just need to get my bag first."

"My truck is parked closer to the stage. I can meet you there in ten minutes. Is that enough time?" Caleb asked.

"That'll be perfect," I said.

Caleb smiled as I walked away. After scanning the surroundings, and nothing seeming out of place, I hurried back to my trailer. After hugging Van and kissing him, I grabbed my bag and headed out the door.

I kept up my guard as I walked across the grassy area of the fairgrounds toward the stage. In the distance, the crime scene came into view. The police had taken away the trailer, but the memory was still fresh in my mind.

I was supposed to meet Caleb in just a couple of minutes, but I couldn't shake the feeling that I should step over there and survey the area. Maybe it would inspire me to paint something, and that painting might offer a clue.

I scanned around to see if anyone was watching me. There was no sign of an Elvis impersonator, or any other celebrity impersonator, for that matter. Other than the ghostly one standing beside me. A few of the craft people milled about, bringing out their items for the day. Which was something I still needed to do.

As I stood in the spot where the trailer had been parked, a chill ran down my spine. Memories of seeing Donald's body flooded back, causing an uneasy feeling within me. My mother would ask why I was putting myself through this. I'm not sure she would understand that I felt I didn't have a choice.

I glanced over to the spot where I'd seen the Elvis impersonator glaring at me. I wished I'd gotten a better view of his face. I checked the time on my phone. Caleb would be worried about me if I didn't hurry up.

The wooded area behind the fairgrounds was a good distance away. I doubted any clues were back there, but nevertheless, I couldn't help but be drawn to it.

With one last glance over my shoulder, I walked to the edge of the woods. A mix of oak, pine, and maple trees filled the space. Stepping under the shade of the branches, the smell of earth encircled me. A shuffling came from my right and my breath caught in my throat. I paused and turned. Seeing nothing, I continued my pursuit of investigating the area.

I needed to hurry because Caleb would be worried about me soon. Standing a good distance away from the clearing where I had entered, I surveyed the ground. I thought maybe the killer had dropped something if he had come this way when he left, or maybe when he entered the area. But that Elvis impersonator had been facing the opposite direction.

What made me think the killer had come from this way? Was a sixth sense pushing me to this spot? Maybe this was part of my psychic ability too.

Something a few steps away caught my attention. Was that paper? I stepped over to the tree, with the crunch of pine branches under my feet breaking the silence around me. Partially hidden under leaves and pine needles was, in fact, a piece of paper.

I reached down and picked it up. The flyer advertised a celebrity look-alike concert. What was this paper doing back here? I flipped it over to see if anything was written on the back. There was a rough sketch of the fairgrounds, with a mark where I was pretty sure the murder victim's trailer had been parked. I knew this because of the relation of the stage position marked on the map and the large oak trees behind the trailer as well. The largest trees had been directly behind Donald's trailer.

"What have you got there?" the voice asked from beside me.

I jumped. "Oh, Donald, you scared me."

"Sorry, dear. I thought you knew I was with you."

To be honest, I'd totally forgotten about his presence. I was so engrossed in finding his killer that I'd forgotten to pay attention to him.

"Again, I ask, what do you have there?" Donald pressed.

"A map. I think someone marked where your trailer was."

"A terrifying thought," he said with a shake of his head.

I had to show Caleb right away. My adrenaline kicked in to overdrive as I hurried out of the isolated and darkened surroundings. I knew the killer truly had been in this spot, and that thought sent a shiver down my spine.

I spotted Caleb standing by the stage, checking his watch. The sunlight highlighted his handsome face.

When I approached, I said, "You're not going to believe this."

Chapter 15

Travel Trailer Tip #15
Spending time alone can be relaxing . . . maybe too relaxing. Set aluminum pie plates around your trailer so you'll know if someone invades your space or disturbs your surroundings.

Caleb dropped me off after we had breakfast. We had a nice time, even though he was a bit agitated with me that I had gone into the wooded area alone, but I pointed out that I'd found a great clue, so it had been worth the risk. The police were going to check the paper for fingerprints. With any luck, they'd find a match.

Even during slow times when no one approached my booth, I still enjoyed my time at the craft fair. I passed the hours by either painting or watching people stroll by. Some people made eye contact and smiled. Others avoided looking my way, as if that would obligate them to buy a piece of art from me.

I used the free time to work on a new piece of art I'd been planning for several days. The image of this piece had flashed in my mind one day last week. Even though I'd driven the stretch of road every day for years, it had only recently come to me that I should re-create the scene on canvas. I'd squeezed varying hues of green on my palette. Stroke after stroke onto the canvas until the vision in my mind had slowly appeared before me, giving a glimpse of what I saw in my mind's eye to the world.

"What do you think, Van?" I pointed toward the canvas.

He barked, his front legs lifting off the ground with the response.

"Thanks, sweetie."

I studied the work. With one last stroke of the brush, I considered the art complete. A landscape that showed the drive down the narrow road to my small cottage surrounded by the tall pines and cedars of the region. The vegetation engulfed my truck as I made the drive every day, like a gentle hug from Mother Nature.

After a good day of sales, I had an added surge of energy. As I put away my paintings, I contemplated my next move. I thought about going back to the wooded area, even though Caleb had told me to stay away. What if there were even more clues? But he had mentioned having the police come back out to look again, so if I went there now, I'd probably be caught. Maybe I should shift gears and think of something else.

Nevertheless, I headed toward my trailer so I could work and maybe clear my mind. Painting always seemed to help me focus. Where was Donald? I was surprised he wasn't currently by my side.

My thoughts came to a screeching halt when someone grabbed me from behind. I couldn't see who it was. Panicked, I tried to tear out of the hold. With one arm wrapped around my waist, the attacker pulled me backward. Their other hand was held in front of my mouth so I couldn't scream out.

No one was around. I scanned the surroundings for any sign of movement, but the trailer site was abandoned. Where was everyone? I tried to break free, but it was impossible. This had to be a man based on the strength and the size of the arms. I was doomed. This was the killer and he'd finally come after me.

"Hey, what's going on over there?" a male voice called from somewhere in the distance.

Whoever had grabbed me let go. I spun around to see who it was, but all I caught was the person's back. He was dressed all in black, even wearing something over his head. A ski mask in the middle of this heat? That had to be unpleasant.

"Celeste!" Donald yelled in a panic, popping up beside me. "I leave your side for two seconds and this is what happens."

The middle-aged man who had yelled ran over to me. "Are you all right?"

"Oh yes, I'm fine," I said, brushing hair out of my eyes.

"She's just lucky," Donald said.

"I don't know who that was, but with a murderer potentially amongst us, you can never be too careful. I called 911 already," the man said.

Everyone would hear about this, and then they'd tell

me that they had warned me. I'd just have to be more careful. Soon the police arrived, and I had to explain exactly what had happened.

"You really should be more careful," Donald warned, as if reading my mind.

I tried to give some description, but I didn't have much to go on. I told them that I assumed my assailant was a man due to the strength of his hold. The middle-aged man who had saved me offered some more details about the attacker's height. But ultimately, he was just a guy wearing all black with his face hidden. There wasn't much the police could do with that.

At least it was over and I was headed to my trailer. I just wanted the safety of familiar surroundings.

When I reached my trailer, I spotted Pierce. The scowl on his face let me know he'd heard about what had happened to me. Even with the pinched brows, he was as handsome as ever. He wore a white dress shirt with the sleeves rolled up, exposing his muscular forearms, a blue tie that made his eyes pop, and dark slacks that hugged his defined legs. He held a file folder, but I didn't ask what was inside. It was none of my business. Though at times I didn't let something like that stop me from inquiring.

"What are you doing here, Pierce?" I asked.

"You need to ask that?" A hint of laughter filled his words.

"I guess not."

"I heard what happened. Naturally, I'm concerned. I had to come by to see if you're all right. How are you? Did he injure you?"

"Just fine. I wasn't hurt seriously," I said.

"She's just lucky." Donald gave a warning shake of his finger.

"I'm really worried about you. Are you telling me the full story?" Pierce asked.

I held up my hands in surrender. "I'm being completely honest. Don't worry, everything will be fine." Unfortunately, I couldn't hide the worry in my voice. At least I'd tried.

"Seriously, Celeste, I know you think trying to investigate is a good idea, but you're wrong."

I ignored his comment. "Speaking of the case, how's it going? Any new leads?"

He ran his hand through his thick hair. "I will admit we're stalled. We checked the cameras around the fairgrounds, but they were faulty and didn't catch a thing."

"You didn't even get fingerprints?"

"Nothing," he said, unable to hide the disappointment in his voice.

I stared out across the field for several seconds before asking, "What about the other case you're working? The stolen artwork?"

"A dead end there too," Pierce said.

He was having a run of bad luck.

"I hope something turns up soon. I know that artwork was worth a lot. Exactly how much was it worth?"

"Five hundred thousand," he said.

Donald coughed, as if choking on the amount.

I let out a whistle. "Well, if I hear anything about it up for sale in the art community, I'll let you know."

"I appreciate that, Celeste. And don't even *think* about hunting for the art. Having you snooping around on one case is bad enough."

"What do you mean, 'snooping on one case?'" I tried to sound innocent.

"We all know you're trying to solve this murder."

"What makes you think that?" I batted my eyelashes.

"Oh, just a hunch, I suppose."

"You're good at hunches," I said.

"Even though the circumstances are bad, I'm glad I got a chance to see you."

I didn't have an answer for that.

Pierce studied my face. "Are you positive you're okay, Celeste?" he asked.

"You know me, I'm always okay. What about you? A murder investigation and the missing artwork? This has to be stressing you out," I said.

"It's tough going, finding the painting." He ran his hand through his hair. "The murder will be easier to solve. At this point, we won't really have any leads in the art theft until someone tries to sell it on the black market."

"I've never understood all that," I said. "Why would someone steal something that was so noticeable? If someone sees the painting, they're going to know it's stolen right away."

"It won't be out in the open, I'm sure," he said. "It'll be in a private collection. Perhaps until someday when they no longer need that cloak of secrecy."

"Are you sure there isn't anything I can do?" I asked.

He smiled, showing his perfect white teeth. "You just can't help yourself, can you?"

I shrugged with a sheepish bite of the lip.

Pierce studied my face as he said, "I kind of hate to admit this, but given your connections to the art world, you might be really good at finding the painting. If you think of anything or hear of anything, let me know."

"No harm in that, right?" I asked.

"Well, this is much better than you trying to solve a murder case."

"I'm careful about the things I do," I said.

"Are you?" he asked with skepticism in his voice.

"Absolutely, tell me more about this painting," I said. "Just so I'll know it if I see it."

He couldn't hold back a smile as he pulled his phone from his pocket. He touched the screen and then showed me. "Here it is."

"Gorgeous. Your work is just as good," Donald said as he leaned close to my shoulder for a glimpse of Pierce's phone.

I flashed a look to Donald, as if to say, *Oh stop, you're embarrassing me.*

The beautiful scene of red and pink roses on a turquoise background almost took my breath away. The intensity of the colors and the strokes of the brush left me awestruck.

"That's it? Wow. I've actually seen it before. Not in person, of course, but I've seen photos of it. The work's stunning. I love the way the artist blended the colors together. I wish I had that kind of talent."

"I think your paintings are phenomenal," Pierce said. "They're different from anything I've ever seen."

There was something special about them, all right. That something special was less about my talent and more about the paranormal. It was sweet of Pierce to offer such a compliment, though, and I appreciated it.

I blushed. "Thank you."

It had been about four weeks since Pierce had gone on his quest to track down that painting. I had to admit I was happy he had returned. Pierce always had a smile on his face and never seemed to let anything get under his skin. It was reassuring.

"As much as I wish this was a social visit, Celeste, there is one other reason I'm here," Pierce said.

He hadn't come by simply to check on me?

"This sounds serious," I said.

"Yes, this does sound serious," Donald chimed in.

I glanced back to see Donald had moved even closer to me. Why couldn't he give some kind of warning when he did that?

Pierce gestured. "Is it all right if we step inside your trailer?"

"Sure," I said, motioning for him to follow.

We stepped inside. Van barely peeked up at us before snuggling down to finish his nap.

"Oh, the detective barely fits in here," Donald said from the corner of my tiny trailer.

The fact that Donald had popped up in the Shasta so quickly gave my heart a jolt, but I didn't flinch to let Pierce know that my ghost had no boundaries.

"Would you like refreshments?" I asked.

"I'm good, Celeste. I hate to ask you this, but it's important." He placed the folder on the counter. "Would you check out a few photos and let me know if you recognize anyone?"

"Oh, is that all? Sure, I can do that," I said.

I was faced with identifying the Elvis in question out

of a lineup of five different Elvis impersonators. Of course, they all looked exactly alike. Plus, I'd seen the Elvis from a distance, so how was I supposed to distinguish any features that might stand out?

Pierce placed the Elvis impersonators' photos in front of me on the table. He wanted me to show him which one I'd seen. "I have no idea."

Pierce sighed. "They all have airtight alibis anyway. One was backstage and many people saw him. The other one we have video of at a store in town. Then another one hadn't arrived yet. Another one wasn't even in the state yet."

If they weren't the killer, then who?

"But I know what I saw," I said.

"I don't doubt that," Pierce said. "I just needed to confirm our suspicion. The killer dressed like Elvis and knew with that many impersonators around, he could easily get away with the murder."

"That he wouldn't be identified," I said.

'Exactly," Pierce said as he picked up the photos.

"So that means we may never find the killer."

"Never finding the killer isn't an option," Pierce said. He was just as determined as me.

"What else can we, er, I mean, *you* do?"

He ignored my slipup and said, "We're searching for DNA evidence. There are other ways." He paused then, noticing the skeptical look on my face. "Just let me do my job and I'll find the killer."

"Yes, let him do his job, Celeste," Donald said.

I never knew when Donald would change his location. Donald listened in to conversations even when I didn't know he was around and that was a bit disconcerting. This was Pierce's way of telling me to stay out of it. That wasn't going to happen. This was personal. Locating the killer was a mission for me. What if someone else was a target? The killer might come back. Specifically, he might come back for me.

I just had to find out who might want Donald dead. If I found out who wanted him dead, I might be able to work backward from there. What other clues could I discover? Maybe if I searched around that trailer, I'd find something. The murder weapon? Where had the wire come from? I had to locate the source of the weapon. There had to be a way for me to solve this crime. Van sat up in bed, as if he'd heard something. One ear perked up and he sniffed the air around him. Did he sense someone outside?

"Hey, how about we take a walk around the midway? We can grab some cotton candy," Pierce suggested. "It'll calm your nerves."

That certainly was a tempting invitation and I supposed I needed a break. Maybe a sugar fix would pick me up. Although I had been trying to avoid junk food while here, one tiny splurge would be okay.

"Sure, that sounds nice," I said.

A huge smile spread across his face and I was even happier with my decision to go with him. Soon we were in front of the cotton candy vendor. I'd probably regret this sugar-fix later tonight when I couldn't fall asleep. The smell of the sweet treat lingered in the air, combined with a hint of the hot dogs and popcorn the vendor sold too.

"How's the painting? Are you able to get anything done with all the action that's been going on around here?" Pierce asked as he handed the man money for the cotton candy.

"I suppose it's been okay. I painted an interesting subject the other day."

"And what's that?" Pierce handed me the fluffy pink candy.

I wasn't sure exactly what to say, but I proceeded to tell Pierce about the painting of Elvis. All the crazy details.

"Interesting," he said as he pulled off a piece of his blue cotton candy and stuffed it into his mouth. "You have a real knack for this psychic stuff. It seems to be getting more amplified by the day."

"I hope it stays where it's at, actually. I can't deal with too many ghosts at once. I have no idea what triggered this in the first place."

"There are many unanswered questions in the universe, Celeste. We'll never know. We just have to go along for the ride and have fun while we're doing it."

I liked the twinkle in his eye when he talked about things like that.

Pierce and I strolled farther away from the cotton candy stand. We were close to the stage. Tonight, the concert wasn't a look-alike show, but a local band. Pierce and I stood there for a few minutes listening to the band.

After a couple of minutes, he asked, "How about we go on a ride?"

"My answer depends on which ride. I'm not good with the scary ones. No heights or plunging to earth in a metal basket."

"We could do the merry-go-round," he said with a wink.

I laughed. "Only if you let me pick out which horse."

"Absolutely," Pierce said. "I wouldn't have it any other way."

Before we had a chance to get on the ride, Pierce received a phone call.

"All right, I'm on my way," he said.

And just like that, our time at the fair had ended. The grim expression on his face let me know he wasn't happy about having to leave. Nevertheless, I knew it was part of his job.

"I got a call about the case, so I need to go check it out," Pierce said.

"About the murder?" I asked. "What happened?"

"Not so fast. I can't tell you what's going on with the case."

"How will I find out if you don't tell me?" I asked.

"That's the point," he said with a laugh. "You're not supposed to find out. Just leave this to me, okay?" Pierce touched my chin with his index finger.

"Okay," I said around a sigh. "But be careful."

"Come on, I'll walk you back to your trailer."

I had hoped to hang around the midway for a while longer, but I knew Pierce wouldn't be okay with that.

He walked me to my trailer door. He wouldn't leave until I had unlocked the door and stepped inside.

"Don't forget to lock the door." He pointed.

"Always," I said.

"Talk to you later?" Pierce asked.

"Sure, I'll talk to you later."

As he walked away, without turning around, he said, "Don't forget to lock your door. Go inside, Celeste."

How had he known I was still standing at the door? Maybe seeing him later would give me a chance to find out exactly why he'd been called to the case. I went back inside, and just as I was going to take out my easel, I heard a male voice from the other side of the door.

"I came as soon as I heard," he said.

I thought I recognized the voice, but I wanted to make sure. I peeked out the window and spotted Caleb. Had he been waiting for Pierce to leave?

When I opened the door, Caleb hurried up the steps, and then he reached out and hugged me. With his strong arms around me, I almost melted right on the spot.

"I'm glad you're here," I said in a low voice, almost whispering in his ear.

He stepped back a bit and searched my eyes. "Are you sure you're all right?"

"Not exactly, but I'm trying my best."

I'd held it together while talking with Pierce. Suddenly, the realization of how close I'd come to becoming the next murder victim hit me.

"Sorry I wasn't here for you." Caleb hugged me again.

"You had no way of knowing that someone would try to attack me," I said.

"Can you tell me what happened?" he asked.

I explained the details, although I hated to upset him more. Maybe I just didn't want to hear how he'd been right and I was wrong to think it was safe around here.

"Did you get a look at the man?" Caleb asked.

"There wasn't time before he attacked me. Plus, he wore a mask."

"Did Pierce say if they'd be able to track him down?"

"I told the police everything, but I don't hold out much hope," I said. "With any luck, they'll listen to me. I'm not the detective on the case, though."

"I'm sure the fact that you're not the detective on the case isn't for lack of trying," Caleb said.

He knew me too well. I wouldn't mention that I'd already been investigating the murder. I just couldn't help myself. A natural curiosity, I suppose. One that could easily get me in trouble.

CHAPTER 16

Travel Trailer Tip #16
If you have other participants, a camping scavenger hunt can be fun. While you're at it, you can hunt for clues.

The next day, when Sammie's number popped up on my phone, I picked up right away.

"Oh, hello," she said in a singsong voice.

I knew by the tone of her voice this meant she had news for me and wanted me to play the guessing game.

"Go on," I said. "You might as well just tell me, because you know I'm terrible at guessing anything."

She laughed. "How did you know?"

"Well, I didn't just meet you yesterday."

"No, you didn't," she said. "It's been how many years?"

"I don't want to admit that out loud because someone might overhear me and realize I'm not twenty-one anymore."

"Oh please, you're still young. We have a lot of years left," Sammie said.

When she said that, the killer came to mind. What if I didn't have a lot of years left? I didn't even want to think about that. I had to push those bad thoughts out of my head. I'd focus on whatever good news Sammie had to share. I knew by her happy tone that it was something juicy.

"Okay, let me have it," I said.

"I guess I'll just come right out with it," she stalled.

"Yes, please do," I said.

"Don't make a big deal out of it, but I have a date." She rushed the words out. She acted as if saying it fast would make the announcement have less of an impact.

This was huge news. And I wasn't supposed to make a big deal out of it? Sammie was extremely particular, and she'd turned down quite a few guys who'd asked her out. Even ones who seemed okay to me. And I was critical of anyone who wanted to go out with her.

"You have a date?" I asked with disbelief.

"I know, I can't believe it either, but I said yes. I just guess I couldn't turn down that sexy smile of his."

"A sexy smile? Well, he sounds interesting. Tell me more about him."

"Well, here's the thing you may not like," she said.

"I'm listening," I said cautiously.

"I believe you may know him."

"Who is it?" I asked.

"He's at the fairgrounds. He's one of the Elvis impersonators."

"What?" I asked with a bit of surprise. "You do realize that an Elvis impersonator is who I suspect of being the killer, right?"

"He's not a killer," she said defensively.

"And you know this how?" I asked.

She paused. "He just doesn't look like a killer."

"Well, no one looks like a killer," I said.

"Some people look like killers," she said. "Like Michael Myers. I mean, come on, he's got killer written all over him."

"That's because he's in a movie where you're meant to know he's the killer," I said.

"Well, there's no way it's this guy, okay?"

"I'm waiting for you to explain this," I said.

"Okay, obviously you already don't like him, but I'm telling you, he's perfectly fine, Celeste."

"What's his name?" I asked.

"Dallas Gunn," she said. "Have you heard of him?"

"I've never heard of him. What else do you know about Dallas Gunn?"

"Well, I know he's from this area and he's really into antiques."

"All right," I said. "He probably just told you that because he knows you have an antique shop."

"No, he mentioned it first."

"That makes it even more suspicious," I said. "What if he's been researching you?"

"Okay, you've been watching way too many of those crime shows. I'm going to have to cut your cable," she said.

"I suppose I'm willing to give him a chance." I sighed.

I was just telling her that because I wanted to meet him. Maybe if I met him, I could figure out more about him and feel him out. There was no way I was going to let my friend go out with someone who might be a potential murderer.

"When do I get to meet him?" I asked.

"Oh, I'm sure you'll get a chance to meet him soon," she said.

"Well, where's he taking you? I have to meet him."

There was another pause.

"You can't seriously think you're going out with him without me meeting him first?" I added.

"Celeste. You're not my parents," Sammie said.

"Well, if I called them, I bet they'd want to meet him too," I said.

She laughed. "You're being way too paranoid."

"When's your date?" I asked.

"In twenty minutes."

"What?" I said, way louder than I had anticipated.

Van barked, as if telling me to tone it down.

"It's the only time he has free," she said.

"That doesn't give me a chance to meet him."

"You can't meet him before we go out. It's not like I need an escort for the date. Maybe I won't even like him, and then there's nothing to worry about."

"There's plenty to worry about," I said.

"Listen, you can text me. I'll let you know after the date's over."

"Where are you going?" I asked.

I knew exactly what I was going to do. I'd follow her to make sure she was okay. I had never done anything like that before, but this was a different circumstance. I mean, I didn't care who she wanted to date. Well, I cared, but it was none of my business until the date involved a potential killer. Then I had to make it my business. She would thank me for it later.

"We're just going to enjoy the fair tonight. Eat junk and go on a few rides. I have to go, Celeste. I promise I'll be fine."

She said that, but it didn't offer me much comfort. I couldn't let this go. I had to do something to protect her.

CHAPTER 17

Travel Trailer Tip #17
Having a travel companion can make the travel trailer time more enjoyable. It can also provide a partner in crime, should you need one.

When I stepped out of the trailer, I didn't expect to bump into Papa.

"How's my Celeste girl doing?" my father asked.

"All right, Papa. What are you doing here? Does Mom know you're here?"

"I didn't tell her. She would only worry. I wanted to check on you." He showed a hint of a lopsided grin.

"I'm fine here, Papa. Don't worry." I locked the trailer door.

There was no way I'd give him the details on what had happened. No need to feed their concern.

"Why don't you load up this trailer and we'll go home? We'll have some chocolate cake."

His offer was tempting. I could walk away from this and all the stress would instantly disappear.

"I can bake you a sugar-free chocolate cake some other day," I said.

"Sugar free? The sugar is what makes it good. But I guess I'll have to take it because your mama will get mad. I'll hitch the trailer to the truck." He gestured.

Uh-oh. That wouldn't end well.

"No, Papa. I can't leave. I'm selling a lot of paintings this time. If I leave now, that would really put a dent in my bank account."

I knew that would get my father's attention. He might not be a rich man, but he worked hard and definitely had an entrepreneurial flair. The fact that I was somewhat following in his footsteps in that regard made him happy and I knew it. Nine-to-five jobs just weren't for us.

"Tell me everything that's going on," he said. "If you're selling paintings, why such a down face? Are you sure you're safe here?"

"You were the one who said there was a police presence and that it's safe."

"Well, I talked with your mama, and I guess I see things her way. I can come stay with you."

There definitely wasn't room in the trailer for more than one adult.

"Things are fine. It wasn't the fact that there's a killer around. I'm kind of upset with Sammie."

"Sammie?" he asked with surprise.

Funny thing, but I never had a problem understanding my father, even if other people didn't quite catch his mumbled words. Yes, he had a Southern accent and was soft-spoken, but I thought that was cute.

"All of a sudden she's enamored with this Elvis impersonator. Which would be great normally, but I'm suspicious of him. What if the police are wrong and all the Elvis impersonators don't have alibis? She's dating a potential killer." I covered my mouth.

Maybe I shouldn't have blurted out that tidbit about the investigation.

My father's normally calm expression turned into one of concern as his brows pinched together. "They don't have alibis? When is the date?" he asked.

"She's going out with him as we speak," I said. "I even told her that I didn't think she should go. But she said I worry too much and that everything was just fine."

"Where are they?" my father asked.

"I think they were walking around the fair," I said.

"Maybe we should check on them to see how they're doing," he said.

"You think?" I said with a smile.

"Absolutely," he said, motioning for me to follow him.

This would be like old times. My father and me alone at the fair. Maybe he could even win me a stuffed animal. Maybe he could have just one treat and we wouldn't tell Mom. If she found out, I'd never hear the end of it.

My father and I stepped away from my trailer and across the way, headed toward the midway. The fair was in full swing. The scent of deep-fried everything wafted through the air.

Sammie wouldn't be happy if she caught us spying on her while she was on a date.

"We have to be sneaky about this," I said.

"I'm an expert at sneaky," my father said.

"I just bet you are," I said with a laugh. "Just try not to be too clumsy tonight, though. That might give us away."

"You know I'll do my best," he said.

As we headed away from my trailer, I pulled out my phone and sent Caleb a quick text. I wanted him to keep an eye out for Sammie and her date too. Maybe he could stop them if he saw them and question the guy. Because I knew Caleb was around the fairgrounds, it was quicker to tell him than to message Pierce about this. After all, I supposed Sammie's date wasn't necessarily part of the murder investigation.

"I just can't believe he's taking her to the concession stand for a date," I said.

"Well, I guess they were already here and enjoying it."

"That's why he should take her somewhere else."

"Do you remember the story of how I took your mother to that fancy restaurant on her birthday? I think she really liked that diner."

"Yes, that was your idea of a fancy restaurant. But she loved it and you had cheeseburgers," I said.

He laughed. "It was fancy for a twenty-one-year-old who had no money."

I patted at my dad's hand. "You got that right, Papa. We just want to follow her and make sure he's on the up-and-up."

"Can you have the detectives do a background check on this guy?" he asked.

"I don't think they can do that," I said. "But I told Caleb about it. I guess as long as she stays out in a public place, she'll be okay."

Up ahead, I spotted Sammie and Dallas as they

strolled along. He wasn't dressed as Elvis, but I supposed I hadn't expected him to be in costume. He wore navy shorts and a white tank top. His short hair was the color of straw. His tan skin made me think he'd spent a lot of time outdoors this summer.

Everything seemed fine between them. They were just walking along, checking out the games and rides. Just normal activities between a couple, but I was on guard for anything suspicious. I caught my dad eyeing a couple of the deep-fried items.

I tugged on his arm. "Keep your mind on the mission."

"They're just so tempting," he said.

I motioned. "They're stopping."

Unfortunately, we had to hide behind the concession stand to watch them. That might make him want to grab an Italian sandwich.

"Focus on them," I said. "No snacks."

"The smell isn't helping," he said.

"We have to get closer so we can hear what they're saying."

They had gotten food and moved over to the picnic benches.

"Wait. I think he's getting up," I said.

Her date moved over closer to the nearby trees. Sammie ate her corn dog and didn't seem concerned about the guy.

"Oh, he's getting on his phone. He's placing a call."

"We have to get over there fast so we can hear."

"But we don't want her to see us either," I said.

My father and I shuffled over to the area, trying to conceal ourselves within the other people in the crowd. Of course, deafening noise surrounded us, with the rides and the people screaming. I hoped we could get close enough so we could hear what Dallas said. My father and I moved closer. We were within earshot.

"Yes, I'm aware," the guy said.

My father and I exchanged a look.

"Well, that's what he gets for taking that gig away from me. I told you, the same thing will happen if anyone tries that again."

What was he talking about? Was he talking about Donald? Sammie's date glanced in our direction. My father and I hunkered down behind the concession stand. A strange noise caught my attention. When I glanced over, I realized my dad was sniffing the air. I'd seen Van do the same thing.

"What do you think he was talking about?" I asked.

"I don't know. It sounded suspicious, though. Maybe we should investigate this more."

"That's a good idea."

"I'm not sure that's a good idea," the male voice said.

I spun around. Donald stood right next to us. I turned to my father, but he was still drooling over the food. How easily he was distracted by delicious-smelling fried stuff on a stick. I contemplated whether I should tell my dad about the Elvis impersonator ghost. Usually, I told him everything, and I thought he was pretty open to that kind of stuff. Still, I was hesitant. Donald eyed me expectantly, waiting for me to acknowledge him.

"Dad?" I said, finally capturing his attention.

He held up his hands. "I was just drooling. I didn't touch."

"No, it's not that," I said. "Do you see anyone standing right next to me?"

He followed the direction of my pointing finger. "I see a lot of people around, honey."

"There's someone in particular standing here." I gestured with a tilt of my head.

With a raised eyebrow, he studied my face. "I'm not sure I understand what you mean."

"You know I told you about my hidden talent for painting, and that sometimes ghosts come through?"

His eyes widened like a light bulb went off in his head. "There's a ghost here?"

"Bingo," I said.

"Who's the ghost?" my dad asked.

"An Elvis impersonator."

Donald wiggled his fingers. "Nice to meet you."

"The one that was killed?" My dad searched for the ghost. "Why is he here? Where's he from?"

"I'm originally from Toledo," Donald answered.

"This is my father, Donald." I gestured.

"Donald?" my dad asked with suspicion in his words. "This is a lot to take in, Celeste. I mean, a ghost? And his name is Donald?"

"Well, my mama didn't think to name me Elvis," Donald said.

I didn't bother to relay the message to my father.

"Anyway, back to the situation at hand." I peeked around the corner to see if Sammie and her date were still there.

Unfortunately, they were gone. I'd allowed myself to become distracted and now I had no idea where she'd gone. She could be in danger.

"Do you know that guy, Donald?" I asked.

"I've seen him around, but that's it," Donald said.

"I have to find Sammie. She left with him." I moved to

the other side of the concession stand to see if I spotted her anywhere.

Sammie was nowhere in sight. I panicked a little.

"Let's go find her," I said.

We made a couple of laps around the midway. I was about to give up when I spotted her out of the corner of my eye. She was on the Ferris wheel with Dallas, laughing at something he'd said.

"She's safe," I said.

Donald, my dad, and I watched as they went round and round on the ride. They had no idea we were watching them. If she spotted us, I would just pretend like we were enjoying the fair. I mean, after all, we were allowed to come here too. I just had to decide what I was going to do when she got off the ride. I supposed we couldn't follow her around for the entire date. Or could we?

"Is there anything we can tell her that will get her to end the date early?" I asked.

"Oh, you could tell her you suspect he's a killer," Papa said.

"That would just get her mad at me. Besides, I kind of already did. She'd just think I was trying to ruin her date because I didn't like the guy."

"Well, isn't that the case?" my dad asked.

"Yes, I suppose it is," I said. "Maybe at the very least I could talk to them to get a better idea whether I trust this guy."

I thought I was a pretty good judge of character. All I needed to do was have a brief conversation with someone and I knew right away whether they were good. Not that I disliked certain people just based on talking to them for five minutes. It was a start, though. Maybe Sammie would think I should mind my own business.

The ride came to a stop. After it swung a few times, Sammie and her date were able to get off. My father and I stepped over to the ride's exit. Sammie and her date walked over.

"I didn't know you guys were here," Sammie said. She was probably suspicious.

"My dad decided to stop by to say hi. I suggested that we walk around and get some treats," I said.

My dad eyed her date up and down. Probably waiting for her to properly introduce him.

"Celeste, this is Dallas Gunn. Dallas, this is my best friend, Celeste, and her dad, Eddie. I was telling you about her. She's the one who does the artwork."

"Oh, right, nice to meet you," he said, sticking out his hand.

He shook my hand and then my father's too. So far, I supposed he was polite enough, but I needed a conversation with him. More than a hello and shaking hands.

"Did you know that Sammie can sing?" Dallas asked.

"Yes, I'm aware," I said.

"He's trying to get me to do a number with him," Sammie said, shaking her head. "I don't think I could ever do that."

"Oh. come on, you know you can." Dallas nudged her with a bump of his hip.

Sammie giggled.

I felt like telling him if she didn't want to do it, he shouldn't make her, but I was just being overprotective. It was occurring to me that he hadn't been featured in the lineup photos Pierce had shown me. That was a red flag.

Donald eyed his competition. "I heard through the grapevine that this guy is terrible. I could sing circles around him. Well, I could have, but anyway, that's beside the point. You're right not to like him, Celeste. I don't like him either. You should tell your friend to get rid of this guy. No reason to hang around with him."

Dallas noticed me watching over his shoulder and glanced in that direction as well.

"I thought I saw someone I knew," I said, trying to smooth out my actions.

He attempted a smile, and I knew Sammie was suspicious too. She probably guessed I was watching a ghost.

"Well, it was nice talking to y'all, but we really need to get going," he said.

Okay, he was rude and pushy.

"Sure," I said. "It was nice meeting you." It was all I could do to say that because I really didn't mean it. Sammie had to know I didn't like the guy.

I hugged Sammie goodbye and whispered in her ear, "Blink if you need me to save you."

She laughed and gestured her hand dismissively. They took off in the opposite direction and an uneasy feeling came over me.

I turned to my father. "Should we follow them more?"

"Well, I would say yes, but I think we're losing our chance," my father said as he pointed behind me.

I whipped around and saw Sammie climbing into a car.

"Oh no," I said, defeated.

"I guess we have no choice but to wait until the date is over," Donald said.

"What if it's too late then?" I asked.

After getting my dad a treat at the concession stand and then saying goodbye, I headed back to my trailer. Of course, Donald walked beside me.

"Well, at least you tried to protect your friend tonight," he said.

"I guess I didn't try hard enough."

"Everything is just fine."

"I guess I'm being too paranoid," I said.

Donald grimaced, letting me know he agreed.

CHAPTER 18

Travel Trailer Tip #18
Don't ignore the things and events around you. Keep your eyes open all the time—except when sleeping, of course.

Throughout the day, while I worked my booth with increasing urgency, I bombarded Sammie with text messages. Naturally, I started to freak out when I didn't hear from her. I wanted to find out if she was still on that date. Mostly, I wanted to make sure she was still alive. I almost called Pierce and Caleb to see if they could track her down. But I knew they would tell me it was too early to file a missing persons report. As I suspected, Sammie had been with Dallas, and she claimed she had forgotten her phone. Now Sammie and I stood in front of my trailer. I held Van in my arms as the last rays of sunshine faded across the sky, leaving streaks of navy and red against the pale blue expanse. Van wiggled in my arms when he spotted a white butterfly floating across our path. He desperately wanted to get at it. His attention was focused on the flying insect, but I was concentrating on getting details from Sammie. I needed to know way more about Dallas. I just couldn't let my best friend hang out with someone who wasn't good for her. I had her best interests to look out for.

Sammie ignored my scrutiny. She wouldn't be able to ignore me forever, though, so I didn't turn my attention away from her. I would force her to acknowledge me. Sure enough, only a few seconds later, she glanced my way.

"What?" she asked.

"You know what," I said. "What's the deal with this Dallas guy? I'm not comfortable with him. I don't trust him."

"Oh, he's fine," she said with a wave of her hand. "You're just being paranoid."

"Well, don't you think I have a reason to feel that way?" I asked.

"He's not a murderer if that's what you think."

"We don't know that for sure. He wasn't even in the lineup. And you're talking about him as if absolutely nothing's wrong."

"As far as I'm concerned, absolutely nothing *is* wrong. I'm a good judge of character. I would know if he was bad."

What could I say to that? There were plenty of people who thought they could judge character, and then they later found out the person was nothing like they thought.

"So tell me, what is it about this guy that has you so enamored?" I asked.

"Have you seen his eyes?" she asked. "I mean, I could just melt into them. He has the deepest, darkest brown eyes. Every time I see him it's like swimming in a pool of chocolate. And the way his mouth turns up at one side and reveals that little dimple. I get light-headed." Sammie swayed a little.

"Well, there has to be something beyond his looks. There has to be another reason why you're so intrigued with him. Tell me more. Persuade me until I like him too."

She shook her head. "Sometimes, I swear, Celeste, you're impossible."

"Why? Because I want my best friend to be happy?"

"You're just being too critical, that's all."

"No, you'll thank me later for doing this. Trust me," I said.

"Did you know that his grandfather played with Elvis's band?" Sammie's voice rose with excitement.

I sighed. "Okay, I admit that's intriguing, and I'd like to hear more about it, but that's not the only reason you like him."

"He graduated from the University of Tennessee with a degree in communications and he's ambitious. He wants to open his own music shop. Plus, we both enjoy antiques. He even knew about that sideboard I got a few days ago. He knew what year it was from. What are the odds of that? What are the odds I'd meet someone interested in antiques as much as I am?"

"I must admit that's good. It's a plus in his column, but he absolutely has to treat you well."

"He opens doors for me, Celeste. I mean, what guy does that nowadays?"

"Caleb and Pierce both do that," I said.

"Well, then, we should consider ourselves lucky, because we've both heard all the stories from other friends about guys and the horrible dates they've gone on. Guys either have trust issues, commitment issues, or they just like the thrill of the chase."

Sammie had a point. We all had those problems with dating. I knew that all too well. If she'd seriously found a good guy, I didn't want her to give that up. But I didn't want her to be hurt either.

"Well, I have a lot of questions for him. Like why he wants to date you. And what he likes about you. And where he sees himself in five years."

"I guess you'll have a chance to ask him that later. But don't bombard him with too many questions, okay?"

"Yeah, okay," I said.

I'd agree to that now, but that didn't mean I'd actually follow through. I would try to sneak in as many questions as possible without upsetting Sammie.

Obviously, I wouldn't be able to talk her out of seeing Dallas again. That meant I had to solve this crime even faster, before something happened to my best friend. I would never forgive myself if I allowed that.

"Everything will be just fine," Sammie said as she touched my hand. "Let's go have fun, okay?"

"Fun? Ha," I said.

"The fair will be over soon and we'll be waiting for next year to come around so we can do this all over again," Sammie said.

"Oh, I don't think I want to do this all over again. It's too stressful," I said.

"Well, I mean do this all over again minus the murder, of course."

"I suppose," I said.

I'd always be worried about when the next murder would occur.

"How about another candy apple? My treat," Sammie said.

"Well, if you're buying . . ."

"By the way, where's the ghost?" Sammie whispered.

"The ghost is right here," Donald answered as he appeared beside her.

"Oh, he's around," I said.

Sammie's eyes widened. "With us?"

"Well, yes, he's nearby."

"I wish I could see him," she said. "I don't like not knowing when someone is standing beside me and eavesdropping."

"I'm not doing this on purpose," Donald said.

I didn't want to be the paranormal translator.

"Speak of the devil," I said.

"What did you say?" Sammie asked.

I pointed down the midway, where Dallas ambled his way over to us. An arrogant air hung around this guy like a dark cloud. I saw none of the qualities Sammie had pointed out.

"Shall we go?" Dallas asked as he took hold of Sammie's arm.

"Hold on just a bit," Sammie said, wiggling free from his hold.

A frown appeared on Dallas's face. I knew he wasn't happy that she was telling him no. Before anyone had a chance to speak, Caleb headed toward us. His attention was focused squarely on Dallas.

Caleb approached him. "I need to ask you a few questions."

Uh-oh. Was he going to arrest Dallas? I hoped Sammie didn't think I'd put Caleb up to it. The men walked toward the edge of the midway.

Sammie and I stood in silence for several seconds. Finally, she asked, "What do you think he's asking him?"

Probably about the murder, but I didn't want to tell her my thoughts. "I'm not sure," I said.

"Dallas looks agitated. Does Caleb thinks he had something to do with the murder?" Sammie sounded worried.

"He probably has to ask everyone in the area," I said. "Especially Elvis impersonators."

"I don't like this," Sammie said. "Can you find out from Caleb what's going on?"

"I can ask him, but he's pretty tight-lipped on this stuff. You know he warns me not to be involved anytime I ask a question. He thinks I'm just trying to get information about the case to solve it."

"Well, isn't that the truth?" Sammie asked.

"Well, yes, but that doesn't mean I should come out and admit it!"

"Maybe Caleb is right. You could be in danger," Sammie said.

"You're one to talk. You're going out with a guy who could possibly be involved."

Sammie slumped her shoulders, defeated.

"I don't mean to upset you," I said.

"I'm just worried, that's all."

"It's good you have a friend who worries about you," Donald said.

Dallas pointed his index finger at Caleb. Caleb didn't back down. Then Dallas turned and walked away.

"That definitely seemed like a heated conversation,"

Sammie said. "Dallas seemed upset. I'll see you in a little bit, okay?"

"I really wish you wouldn't go," I called out.

She waved and walked away. Sammie had a stubborn streak and always did exactly what she wanted. There was no talking her out of it.

"What can I do?" I asked.

Donald shrugged. "I wish I had an answer for you."

Caleb locked eyes with me as he walked toward me. "Is everything okay?" he asked.

"I should ask you the same thing. That conversation back there with Dallas—it didn't go well, I suppose?"

"No. He doesn't want to answer any questions. He thinks we're putting too much heat on him." Caleb used air quotes around the word "heat."

"Do you suspect him of murder? I'm really concerned because Sammie has been spending a lot of time with him," I said.

"I can't rule him out. Everyone is a suspect," he said.

Did that mean even *I* was a suspect?

"That's what I was afraid of. She went to talk to him, but I'd rather she stayed away from him. She won't listen to me, though."

"So that's another thing you all have in common?" Caleb asked.

"Funny," I said with a smile.

"It's true," he said.

"What can I do to get her to stop seeing this guy?"

"Nothing. All you can do is be watchful."

"Well, don't worry. I'm working on figuring this out," I said.

"You know, maybe we should just hire you for the police force." Caleb bit back a smile.

"That's not a bad idea," Donald said.

"Maybe I'll give that some thought," I said around a laugh. "In the meantime, I have some paintings to finish up before the show tomorrow, so I guess I'd better get back."

"Can I interest you in a candy apple?" Caleb asked with a wink. He knew my weakness.

"Only if you get me one of the ones with the nuts," I said.

"It's a deal," he said.

He held out his hand and I took it. We walked over to the food counter. Caleb was being more and more affectionate, and I wasn't pushing him away from doing it.

While he ordered two candy apples for us, I took the opportunity to scan the midway again for signs of anything nefarious. I wasn't exactly sure what I was looking for. It wasn't as if the killer would just pop out and say, *Hey, over here. Here, it's me. I'm the killer.*

"What are you up to, Celeste?" Caleb asked, snapping me back to reality.

"Just enjoying the scenery, I suppose," I said as I took the apple from his hand. "Thank you."

Caleb and I walked down the midway, eating. Nuts from the treat dropped to the ground with each step. We were too busy enjoying the apples to say a word. Maybe that was for the best, because he'd just tell me to stay out of the investigation. But I did enjoy our other talks. The times when we discussed our art, our dogs, Aunt Patty's cheeseburgers, and the other things we liked.

Again, I became distracted when I spotted Kaye. I'd wanted to talk with her since I'd first seen her and this was my chance. How would I explain that to Caleb? I could tell him she was a friend, but what if he knew differently?

"I need to go to the ladies' room. I'll be right back," I said.

By all appearances, it seemed as if Kaye was headed that way too. This might work out perfectly. Caleb wouldn't be able to say that I had lied.

"I'll wait here for you," he said.

Before he realized what I was up to, I took off toward the area where I'd just seen Kaye. She was nowhere in sight, though. I needed to track her down, even though I wasn't sure what I'd do if I found her. After that awkward first encounter, this would probably be even weirder. I weaved around a group of people and then spotted her up ahead. Thank goodness. Unfortunately, she wasn't going to the restroom.

She'd just disappeared into the fun house. Or as the colorful blinking lights indicated, Wacky Shack Funhouse. I didn't have time for a trip through a mirrored maze! But it seemed to be my only option.

I rushed over to buy tickets for entry. I handed my money to the bearded man selling them, then raced up to the young man working the entrance. After feverishly shoving my admission toward him, I stepped inside.

Flashing lights guided me into the depths of this so-called fun house. I met my reflection. As I turned, I was startled by the duplications of myself that splintered off in every direction. I pushed my hands forward so I could feel whether I was about to smash into a mirror. Realizing there was a wall in front of me, I moved to the left and inched my way through.

Tinkling music sounded from all around, reminiscent

of a tune from a horror movie I couldn't place. I assumed a clown might pop out of a box at any moment. I found myself becoming more anxious with every note. The anticipation that someone might jump out in front of me was almost too much to handle. Images of manic-looking clowns covered the walls that didn't have mirrors. Or were those mirrors and the clowns were real? Fear spiked inside me. *Get ahold of yourself, Celeste.*

The lights seemed to flash faster, making things appear even more distorted. Up ahead, I spotted the back of Kaye. I moved in that direction, feeling my way through and seeing my clone at each step. I'd almost made it to what I thought was the end when I spotted a dark figure. He was dressed all in black. I caught his reflection out of the corner of my eye, where he stalked like a shadow. The person was making his way toward me. My heart thumped wildly in my chest. I had to get out of there. Talking to Kaye was no longer my mission. Just staying alive and getting out of the place was now my main goal.

I smacked into the wall and groaned. Checking over my shoulder, I caught a glimpse of the figure headed toward me. I frantically reached around in front of me and pushed. The door opened and I spilled out into the summer air. I gasped and raced to my right, desperate to get away from the area. Kaye was nowhere in sight. I'd put myself in danger for nothing.

When I rounded the corner, I spotted her. She stood next to a line of trash cans. It would have been the perfect chance to speak with her, but Caleb was nearby. He would notice me. I slipped behind the funnel cake stand. The scent of vanilla and cinnamon wafted in my direction, making my mouth water. My dad would have loved this spying assignment.

How long would I stand and watch her? Caleb checked his watch. He would probably come searching for me soon. Kaye's posture stiffened. She focused straight ahead. When I followed her stare, I spotted Dallas. He was headed her way. They knew each other too?

Dallas stepped up to Kaye. He held a small white bag in his hand. They started talking, but of course, I had no idea what they were discussing. This would drive me crazy, wondering how and why they knew each other. My worry for Sammie increased. This guy was definitely trouble.

As they continued their conversation, Dallas shoved his hand into the white bag and pulled out a doughnut. My eyes widened. He took a big bite. Jelly from the doughnut spilled onto his white shirt. He didn't seem to notice. Was that blueberry jelly? Just the kind of doughnut that had been in Donald's hand.

After a few more seconds, he finished the doughnut and tossed the bag into the trash. At least he hadn't littered. Even a potential killer liked to keep the area neat and tidy. Dallas walked away and Kaye remained in the same spot. I desperately wanted a peek at that bag.

My phone alerted me to a text. Caleb had asked if I was okay.

Be right there. I added a smiley face, hoping he wouldn't be suspicious.

He had no idea I could see him from where I stood. Kaye waved at someone. Checking over my shoulder, I spotted Justin Blackburn headed her way. A flashback of overhearing him talking to his girlfriend came to mind. He'd certainly seemed guilty of something. I eyed him up and down. He wore all black. This sent a shiver down my spine. Had he been the one inside the fun house?

Once the couple met up, they walked away. This gave me a chance to dig through the trash. I had to hurry so that Caleb wouldn't catch me. Explaining to him why I had my hand in a trash can wouldn't be easy. Once at the receptacle, I glanced around. With no one watching me, I stuck my hand in and pulled out the bag. The bakery's name, the Bear Claw Bakery, was on the bag. I knew where that place was. It seemed a visit was in order.

Something else on the bag caught my eye. In black ink was a sketch of a skeleton. The drawing was nothing special, meaning the artist was just mediocre. But the thing I found most interesting was the signature underneath the little sketch. Justin Blackburn. Apparently, he liked to doodle. Why had he drawn on Dallas's bag?

Chapter 19

Travel Trailer Tip #19
Having visitors in your trailer can be nice. Offer them lemonade and cookies while you ask them questions about the murder you're solving.

After Kaye and Justin walked away, I joined Caleb again. He never mentioned the length of time I'd been gone, but I knew he must be a little curious. We spent another thirty minutes walking the midway, but I didn't spot Dallas, Kaye, or Justin again.

As soon as I arrived back at my trailer and said good night to Caleb, I went inside and called Sammie. She was seriously worried that Dallas might not be the right guy for her.

"This might be another strange question, but does Dallas draw or do any painting?" I asked.

"No. As a matter of fact, when he found out you're an artist, he mentioned he's terrible at it," Sammie said. "Why do you ask?"

"Just a few things I'm working on. I hope you'll listen to my warning."

"Okay. I'm starting to see your point, Celeste. I'll put distance between us and hope he doesn't reach out again. I just can't believe this. He seemed like such a nice guy." Disappointment filled her words.

That made my heart hurt for Sammie.

"I'm sorry, sweetie. I know it's disappointing. But it's better that you figured this out now, early on, before things get serious."

I was awash with relief at this turn of events. At least I knew my best friend was safely out of harm's way.

When a knock came at my trailer door, my heart instantly sped up. With a killer running around, any noise like that would certainly get me off guard and cause panic.

I moved over to the little window so I could peek outside. If it was someone I didn't know, there was no way I'd answer the door. I felt trapped in this tiny space. I checked outside and recognized the woman. Relief came over me.

Madame Gerard had come to visit. And although it was a bit of a shock, I was glad to see her. I hurried over to the door and opened it up.

"Madame Gerard, what a lovely surprise. Is everything all right?"

"I'm not sure. I came to talk to you. It's an emergency."

"What's wrong?" I asked. "Would you like to come inside?"

She scanned around, as if somebody might have followed her or might be watching us. "Yes, that would be nice."

Madame Gerard climbed the trailer steps and then stood in my tiny space. With her height, I instantly felt as if the room was even smaller. It was just me and Van in here most of the time. Well, also a ghost a lot of the time. I'd met Madame Gerard a short time ago when Sammie had taken me to have my fortune read. Little had I known then that she would play a bigger part in my life.

Blond hair tumbled in waves over her shoulders. Her long, black skirt and white blouse fit slightly askew on her body, as if she'd dressed in a hurry. However, her makeup still seemed immaculately applied. She must have a great setting spray. Were her eyelashes real or fake? *Focus, Celeste, focus.*

"Would you like to have a seat?" I gestured toward one of the stools.

"Thank you."

"How about something to drink?" I asked.

I was trying to be a gracious host, but I really wanted to know about the emergency.

"I'm fine, thank you." Madame Gerard waved her hand. "I just had a vision. Something came to me and I instantly knew I had to tell you. I feel you are in danger."

"Well, you were spot-on with that one. There's been a murder here and a killer is on the loose. Not to mention someone did attack me."

"Oh no." Her gold bangle bracelets jingled with her wild arm gesture. "I was afraid of that."

My heart beat faster as I thought about her vision. A warning. Like I already wasn't panicked enough.

"What did you see?" I asked.

"I saw a man coming for you. He came to your trailer. I think you need to get out of here." Madame Gerard moved over to the window and peeked out of the blind's slats.

"Did you get a look at the man?" I asked. I tried to stay calm to get as much information as possible.

"Okay, maybe this sounds crazy, but . . ." She paused, obviously trying to decide whether she should share the full details.

I had to know. No way could she keep this from me.

"I think he was dressed like Elvis."

"It doesn't sound crazy," I said. "I fully expected you to say that, actually."

"What do you mean?" she asked. "Did you see something too?"

"There are several Elvis impersonators here at the fair. I think one of them is the killer. The person who was killed was another Elvis impersonator."

"What's going on here?" she asked, perplexed.

"I don't know, but hopefully, it's something I'll find out soon."

"Don't do that. Get out of here before it's too late," she said.

"I can't do that. I have to solve this so no one else gets hurt."

"But you realize what I just told you. That you're in danger?"

"Yes, I realize that," I said. "But it's the chance I have to take. I appreciate you wanting me to be cautious. I will be, I promise. And there are police everywhere if that makes you feel any better."

"You're not listening to me," she said.

"Is there anything else you can tell me about what you saw? Maybe a certain area I should avoid?" I'd take any little detail I could get, but I couldn't just leave the fair right away. I certainly wouldn't tell Pierce and Caleb about this. They were close to having me arrested just to get me away from here.

I suspected my parents would probably try to come up with a reason to get me away from here too. I just couldn't stand having unanswered questions. I had to know the truth, had to help others before they were killed, just like Donald.

"Well, like I said, I think the person was coming near your trailer," she said.

I was almost afraid to ask what she saw this person doing. Obviously trying to kill me, but maybe if I knew how, I could be prepared. I'd know when to watch for the attack.

When a knock sounded at the door, Madame Gerard and I both froze.

"Are you expecting someone?" she asked with a hint of panic.

"No, I'm not," I whispered.

I hoped it was either Pierce or Caleb, but Madame Gerard seemed worried that it might be the killer she had envisioned.

"Don't worry, I'm sure it's nothing," I said, trying to sound brave.

Where was Donald when I needed him? He could tell me who was at the door. I wasn't sure I'd be able to peek out to see who was out there now that it had grown dark outside. Why had Madame Gerard waited until it was dark to come around? I'd worry about her walking out there alone when she went home.

It didn't matter who was at the door because I'd already made up my mind I was calling Caleb. I'd have him escort Madame Gerard back to her vehicle. Nevertheless, in the meantime, I'd see if it was either detective.

As I hurried to the door, I crossed my fingers it was either Pierce or Caleb. When I peeked out the door, I saw no one there. That sent a panic throughout my body.

"Who is it?" Madame Gerard asked.

"I don't see anyone at the door," I said.

"I was worried about that," she said.

"You think this is the killer you saw? Is he here to find me?" I asked.

"I'm not sure what to think, but the possibility is very real." The ominous tone of her words hung in the air.

"All right, we just have to stay calm," I said. "I'll call the police and have them check things out. I also want them to walk you back to your vehicle. There's no way you're walking around here alone, not after what's happened."

I thought she might argue with me about this but, thank goodness, she didn't say a word. I pulled the phone from my pocket and dialed Caleb's number. Unfortunately, he didn't answer.

"No answer," I said. "But I'm sure he'll call back soon. He always does."

I debated if I should call Pierce to see if he could come over here. Though he'd wonder why I hadn't called him first and then, if Caleb called back, he'd wonder why I called Pierce. I was torn between the two men. Another knock sounded at the door. Fear spiked and coursed through my body. This was almost too much to handle.

Without warning, Madame Gerard jumped up from the stool and raced over to the door.

"Where are you going, Madame Gerard? Is something wrong? Did you have another vision?" I asked.

She remained silent as she opened the door and hurried outside into the dark night. She could easily meet up with the killer. There was no telling where someone might lurk, hiding behind any object and waiting for the chance to attack. It was too dark to see.

I raced out the door, closing it behind me so Van wouldn't get out, and then headed after her.

"Stop! I have to call somebody to walk you to your car. It's too dangerous," I called out.

Madame Gerard kept running, as if she was completely freaked out. She rounded the corner and I lost sight of her, which made me even more panicked.

"Madame Gerard?" I called out.

It was no use. She wouldn't stop. I couldn't believe she'd taken off like that. She was always so calm and collected, but something had completely spooked her. I rounded the corner but didn't see her. My heart was ready to pound out of my chest—where had she gone? When I ran to the edge of the trailer, I saw her. Then, from my left, I spotted someone coming out from behind one of the trees. Even though the dark of night surrounded us, I could still see that he wore all black and a black mask over his face.

He wrapped his hand around her mouth. She tried to scream, but his hand muffled the sound.

"Hey, take your hands off her," I yelled out.

Instantly, the man released her and took off running. Miraculously, I'd scared him away.

I raced over. "Are you okay, Madame Gerard?"

She was scared speechless. All she did was nod, indicating that she was fine.

"Why don't you come back to the trailer with me?" I said. "We'll call the police. We have to tell them what happened."

Unfortunately, she didn't listen to me again and took off running toward her vehicle. At least I had her in my line of vision and I saw that she actually reached her car. She jumped inside and cranked the engine. And then sped away with a squeal of the tires.

As I stood out here alone, my fear spiked. I turned and ran toward my trailer. Even though Madame Gerard had gone, I was still calling Caleb. When I got inside, relief washed over me, and I wiped the sweat from my hands on my pants before pulling out my phone.

I hadn't even gotten a chance to dial the number when my phone rang. I was so startled, I almost dropped the thing. But at least I was back in my trailer, with the door locked and secure. When I checked the number, I saw it was Pierce calling. He would recognize the stress in my voice right away. I supposed there was no point in hiding what had happened.

"I'm glad you called," I said when I answered.

"What happened?" Pierce asked.

"Madame Gerard was just here. While we were talking inside my trailer, someone knocked on the door. For some reason, she panicked and took off. When I ran after her, a man grabbed her."

"Is she okay?"

"Yes, I think she's fine. I yelled at the guy and he let her go. I was surprised by that."

"Where is she? Are you all right?" he asked.

"I'm okay. I'm in my trailer, with the door locked, of course. She got in her car and took off. I'm worried about her. Could you send someone over to check on her?" I asked.

"I'll absolutely have someone check on her."

"You know, considering she had that break-in once, I worry about her."

"It's understandable that you're upset. I'm worried about you too. You're right there in the middle of all this, and I told you it was dangerous. We both know that you're not exactly the most cautious person."

"What do you mean? I'm perfectly cautious," I said.

"You ran outside in the middle of the night after hearing a strange noise and an attacker was there."

"Yes, but I'm safe now, and I'm in my trailer with the door locked. So, see, I was cautious."

I knew he was thinking this over, trying to find an argument against it, but he had to admit I was right. Sure, it had been a bit risky, I would admit that, but nonetheless I'd made it out of the situation unscathed.

"I'm on my way there," Pierce said. "Just stay inside the trailer until I get there. Don't open the door for anyone."

He'd barely finished the sentence when a knock sounded at the door. I raced over and peeked out the window to see who had knocked this time. The light from Caleb's phone as he held it in front of him showed his face as he stood in front of the door. He glanced over and noticed my face peeking out.

"What about opening the door for Caleb?"

"I'm on my way," Pierce said.

After ending the call, I let Caleb in. I glanced around into the dark night, but there was no sign of the strange man who had attacked Madame Gerard. The blinds on the door rattled as I slammed it shut. Hurriedly, I locked the door behind us. I tried to catch my breath, but it felt as if all the air had been sucked out of the room.

"What's wrong with you?" he asked.

"I think the killer attacked Madame Gerard. It's all such a blur. It happened so quickly."

"Okay, just calm down and tell me exactly what happened," Caleb said

Once again, I relayed the whole story. Caleb watched me intently.

"She told me that I was in danger, and then all of a sudden she was attacked, and when I yelled at the guy, he ran away."

"I've been telling you that this is dangerous and yet you continue to investigate. When will you learn to stay out of it?" His face was tight with intensity.

Okay, he was kind of hurting my feelings. I thought I was a good investigator. And I had to check into this murder. I mean, my painting had summoned the victim! I couldn't just ignore my psychic ability.

Caleb must have noticed the expression on my face. He came over, placed his hands around my arms, and gazed into my eyes. "Celeste, I'm sorry. I didn't mean to hurt your feelings. It's just that I care about you more than I think you know."

My heart sped up and my body tingled with the words. How much did he care for me? I wasn't sure I knew. Maybe I should pay more attention and find out.

Caleb continued, "I have no doubt that you can solve this or any other crime you put your mind to, but I don't want you hurt. If solving it means you're going to be in jeopardy, I don't want it to be solved by you."

He searched my eyes, hoping I understood. Deep

down, I understood how he felt, but I was stubborn. I knew I could handle myself. After all, he was doing the exact same thing and I wasn't worried about him, so what made it any different? The sooner he realized it, the better off we'd be.

Soon, another knock came at the door.

"This is getting out of hand," Caleb said as he went over to the window to check.

A second later, he moved over and opened the door.

"How is she?" Pierce asked.

"She's fine."

They spoke as if I couldn't answer for myself. Pierce stepped into the trailer. Other officers were moving around outside, shining flashlights that dotted the darkness with a white glow.

"We're checking the perimeter to see if we can find any sign of the perpetrator," Pierce said.

"It's getting crowded in here," Donald said.

He stood by the door with a confused expression on his face. I couldn't talk to him with Caleb and Pierce here. They already thought I was kooky enough.

"Can you tell me anything else that might help us locate this person?" Pierce asked.

"Nothing that I can think of," I said as I pushed the hair out of my eyes. No doubt I was a mess after chasing the man who'd attacked Madame Gerard. Part of my hair had fallen from my ponytail, and I had paint all over my shirt from the art I had worked on earlier in the day. But my appearance was the least of my worries. Just staying alive was what I had to focus on.

I racked my brain, trying to come up with something that would help Caleb and Pierce locate the attacker. I felt useless, failing with my so-called detective skills. I should be able to think of something that would help. Why hadn't I paid more attention? It had all happened so quickly, though. I supposed I really had no time to scrutinize the attacker's appearance. I'd just been worried about Madame Gerard's safety.

I replayed the entire scene in my mind, hoping that would spark a memory. It played out just like a movie, but nothing new revealed itself to me.

"Is everything all right?" Caleb asked, snapping me back from my musings. I'd been completely lost in the scene.

"Yes, I'm fine," I said. "Just trying to remember."

"Don't stress about it too much," Pierce said.

How could I not stress when I knew the killer was out there somewhere? He was just waiting for the perfect opportunity to attack.

Chapter 20

Travel Trailer Tip #20
Make sure to visit the local area around your campground. You never know where you may find out something about a suspect.

I had to pay a visit to Madame Gerard. I hoped she could give me more information about the murder investigation. I knew she couldn't just gaze into her crystal ball and give me the identity of the perpetrator, but she was oftentimes able to get little clues that might help. It certainly couldn't hurt. If a ghost managed to come through and give her a message, well, that would be even better. Because even though I had the ghost of the victim at my disposal, he didn't seem to know much of anything, besides his favorite Elvis songs.

Pierce had told me that Madame Gerard had made it home safely after the attack, but I had to see her for myself. I hopped into my truck with Van by my side and headed toward her house.

As I walked across the parking lot toward my truck I

spotted Justin's car. Naturally, curiosity got the better of me. I looked around to see if anyone was watching me. Perhaps I'd just take a quick peek inside to see if there was anything interesting.

I hurried over to the car because I wanted to get away as soon as possible before being caught. I had no idea when he might show up. If he caught me, he'd definitely wonder why I'd been looking in his car.

Unfortunately, when I tried the doors, they were both locked. Cupping my hands around my eyes, I peeked into the car. Nothing of interest in the front seats except for food wrappers. But in the back seat, I found something curious. Paintings. I couldn't tell for sure, but it looked like Justin's signature at the bottom. So he was an artist? I hurried away from the car with no definitive clues, but a bad feeling had settled in the pit of my stomach. I felt as if I was on the cusp of something, but I had no idea what just yet.

The short drive to Madame Gerard's place gave me a chance to enjoy the beautiful landscape I called home. Driving down the main drag in town, I soaked in the peaks and the forest scenery beyond all the shops and entertainment. I never tired of having the lush, green, tree-covered, cloud-topped mountains as the backdrop of my life.

Mingled in were all the tourist attractions. The Gatlinburg Space Needle was on the right, with an observation tower that overlooked downtown and the Smoky Mountains. Glass elevators carried people all the way to the top. A bit farther was the Ripley's Believe It or Not! Museum. The large, red-brick building appeared as if it might be falling apart, but it was designed that way on purpose.

Soon, I pulled into Madame Gerard's driveway. I parked the truck, picked up Van, and headed toward her front door. A neon sign flashed Open, casting an eerie red glow across the walkway that led toward her front door.

The cute white house had black shutters and pretty red flowers in planters out front by the steps. The only thing that stood out from the other houses around was the giant sign with a palm on it in the front yard.

MADAME GERARD
PSYCHIC READINGS AT
YOUR DISPOSAL

I stepped up to the door and pushed the bell. A few seconds later, I got the sense that someone was watching me. When I glanced to my right, I spotted it, just a peek of her blue eyes as she peered out at me from the sliver at the window not covered by the curtains. Then, seconds later, I heard her unlocking the door. I guessed she had about ten variations of latches, bolts, and padlocks, but I'd never actually counted. What was she trying to keep out or keep from getting out?

Cracking the door just a hint, Madame Gerard eyed me without speaking.

"Is it all right if I come in for a reading?" I asked.

A faint smile appeared. "Certainly. You're welcome anytime, Celeste."

Madame Gerard stepped to the side and opened the door wider. With a sweeping motion, she gestured for me to enter. It had taken her a while, but she had definitely warmed up to me over the last few months. Madame Gerard appeared standoffish to everyone. I didn't take it personally. It was just her way, which was kind of odd, considering she worked with the public.

"What brings you by?" Madame Gerard asked.

"I wanted to make sure that you got home safely and that you're okay."

She released a deep breath, as if she'd been holding in all that worry and finally was able to release it. "Yes, yes, I'm good. I sense you need something else."

"Well, I'm glad you're okay. I guess there was one other thing. I wondered if you could do a reading for me?"

"Of course." She gestured toward the room to the left. "Please come inside."

I stepped in, noticing the white fabric that was draped over a large, round table in the middle of the room. Chairs surrounded the table with a crystal ball in the middle. Candles flickered all around. I had no idea if she could really see into that crystal ball, but it made a nice centerpiece, adding the ambience customers probably expected. Nevertheless, I knew she had some abilities because she'd told me things that were true.

I took a seat across from where I knew Madame Gerard would sit. She had a special chair with her name written on the back. I put Van down on the chair across from me. He curled up in a ball to take a nap. We hadn't been here that often, but he already knew the routine.

Madame Gerard stepped across the room. The golden bangle bracelets on her wrists jingled as she picked up a deck of cards. Seconds later, she sat down across from me. She shuffled the cards, then placed them on the table, concentrating on the back of each one. She finally flipped a few over and studied the first card. She tapped her finger against it.

"Do you see anything?" I asked, breaking the silence.

She didn't answer. I supposed I was expected to keep quiet until she spoke. Maybe I was breaking her concentration.

"Uh . . ." she said as she moved on to the next card.

That didn't sound good. I had hoped for something more along the lines of, "Oh, how nice," or "How exciting," or "Good news." Sadly, those words hadn't come from her mouth. She remained quiet. The anticipation was getting to me. I thought I might burst out soon if she didn't respond. A grim expression appeared on her face as she moved to the third and final card. She tapped it with her finger. In my opinion, she was staring at it much longer than I thought necessary. Just when I thought I couldn't keep my mouth shut a moment longer, she turned her attention to me.

She stared at me straight in the eye. "Yes, I do see something in the cards for you."

"And what is it?" I asked. Maybe I didn't want to know after all. Van raised up and stared at her.

"I see that there's a place you should go," she said.

My eyes widened. "Do you know where?"

I peeked at the scene as if I would be able to distinguish a location, but the figures on the cards gave me absolutely no clue.

"A musical show," she said. "Someone who's performing in a musical show. Does that sound familiar?"

"Well, I've been surrounded by Elvis impersonators and other imitation celebrities all week long, so it has to be something at the county fair."

"No, I think it's something different. Though I don't know what it would be. Maybe you should check with some of the other performers. If they have other venues."

"Is that all you see?"

"Well, also that you should be extremely careful. And something about a ghost?"

"I'll be careful," I said. "There's another ghost around, but he's not with me today." I checked over my shoulder to make sure Donald hadn't popped up unbeknownst to me. There were no ghosts in sight.

"I think he could help you, but I'm not sure how. Just keep pushing him to do something."

Well, that was easier said than done, I thought. "Thank you for the information."

"You know I'm here to help you anytime."

She was so much more talkative than when I'd first come to see her. I was glad of that. I considered her a friend and I hoped she felt the same way about me. I was just ready to get up from the table when all the candles flickered. They were about ready to extinguish on their own when a chill came over the room.

Goose bumps appeared on my arms. Madame Gerard checked all around, frantically searching for the cause. My heart sped up. It felt as if someone else had stepped into the room with us. I turned my attention to the doorway, wanting to see if Donald had appeared. There was no sign of him. I sensed something different, and not good either. A bad spirit. This made me want to get up and run, but I also didn't want to leave Madame Gerard alone. A noise came from the back of the house. Madame Gerard and I exchanged a look.

"Is someone else in the house with you?" I asked.

"I need to check it out." She stood from the chair.

"I'll go with you," I said.

She didn't argue. Madame Gerard and I walked toward the back. The kitchen was located at the rear of the home. More noise came from that area, like footsteps.

I hoped someone hadn't broken in, because I wasn't certain what I would do to defend us. Trying to be brave, I stepped in front of Madame Gerard.

"Let me go first," I said.

"Be careful," she said.

When we reached the kitchen door, I put Van down on the floor in case someone attacked me just as I opened it. I knew he would stay put on the floor. I placed my hand on the swinging door and eased it open ever so slightly. So far, there was no sign of anyone. I opened the door a bit more and stuck my head around, checking to the left and to the right. No one was there. I opened the door wider and stepped inside, motioning for Madame Gerard to join me.

"No one's in here," I said.

She followed me into the room as I moved over to the back door. Perhaps someone had been there but had left when they heard us. However, I checked the door and it was locked many times. I gazed out the window into the backyard. Nothing.

What if the killer had followed me to Madame Gerard's house? I hated the thought that I might have brought danger to her, but it was a possibility, considering I was almost positive the killer knew I was searching for him. It would only be a matter of time until he came after me. He would do anything to stop me from discovering his identity and telling the police. Still, I had to keep Madame Gerard calm.

"Everything is fine," I said. "It was probably just the house settling."

Madame Gerard didn't seem convinced about that. Nevertheless, she nodded and accepted my explanation.

Maybe it really had been a ghost. The one that had stepped through from her crystal ball.

I moved back into the parlor and picked up Van. "I think it's time for us to leave."

Madame Gerard walked me to the door. With all the locks she used to secure her premises, I assumed she'd be safe, but I still had an uneasy feeling about the noise we'd heard.

After leaving her place, I headed straight for the next location I hoped would provide some insight into the murder. The small white building housing Bear Claw Bakery was set to the side, away from the other shops in town along Main Street. Parking spaces lined the front, adjacent to the quaint patisserie. Bear Claw Bakery was written in pink letters on the white sign above the door. Considering the number of bears in Gatlinburg, the name was apropos.

"Do you really think going to the bakery will help you get a clue to solving my murder?" Donald asked as he materialized beside me in the truck.

I made a left turn onto Main Street. "It certainly can't hurt to ask."

"No, I suppose not," he said as he tapped his fingers against the seat.

I knew he was anxious, and I was trying to help him out as much as possible. This was the only thing I knew to do. After I found the bag Dallas had tossed in the trash after eating a doughnut, I figured I should go to the shop to ask them about him. They might remember him if he made it a habit of buying that specific kind of doughnut. Maybe that was just the clue I needed to prove he was the killer. I pulled up in front of the bakery, whipped the truck into a spot, and hopped out.

Donald hurried along beside me. "What are you going to say to them?"

"Well, as I said before, I don't make plans. I'll just wing it."

"You really should look into thinking things out a bit more," Donald said.

"Hey, reserve your criticisms for when you have better ideas!" I said as I opened the door.

I hoped no one noticed that I was talking to myself, but I didn't have the energy to pretend to be on my phone. They'd just have to think I was crazy, I supposed. The smell of yeast and icing drifted across the air, making my mouth water. Perhaps I could pick up a doughnut for myself.

"Oh, I think I'm getting dizzy," Donald said. "I can't handle all this deliciousness in one spot."

Maybe it was a bad idea to have him along. I'd forgotten how much he loved doughnuts, right until his dying bite.

I needed to hurry and get Donald out of here before he had a meltdown. I had no intention of finding out exactly what a ghost meltdown was like.

A young brunette with her hair in a braid was behind the counter. She met my gaze and smiled as I stepped up to the counter. "May I help you?" she asked in a cheerful tone.

I glanced at the glass display case. "I'd like a glazed doughnut, please."

"Just one?" Donald asked in a loud voice. "You need to get one for me too."

I didn't want to remind him that he couldn't eat the treat. However, I humored him and said, "And a jelly doughnut, please."

The girl started retrieving the doughnuts. In the meantime, I pulled out my phone so I could show her the photo of Dallas that I'd taken.

When she placed the bag of doughnuts on the counter and gave me the price, I showed her the phone. "Do you recognize this guy?"

She looked at the screen and then studied my face. "Yes, I've seen him. He's a regular in here."

Bingo.

"Does he happen to like blueberry jelly doughnuts?" I asked.

Her face scrunched up in a frown. "Yeah, he always gets them."

Exactly what I'd thought. Her answer let me know this was something that could lead back to Dallas as the killer.

"Thank you," I said as I marched out of the bakery.

"Don't get too cocky. That doesn't prove anything," Donald said as I got into my truck. "Are you going to eat that doughnut?"

Chapter 21

Travel Trailer Tip #21
Meet your neighbors. They might offer interesting tidbits that will turn your investigation in a new direction.

Every time I sold at a craft fair, I liked to check out the other vendors. With such a wide variety of items, how could I resist? One of the neighboring vendors had agreed to watch my booth while I walked around the grounds. She seemed nice enough, and it turned out that she knew my grammy, so I trusted her.

I never knew what kind of treasure I'd find. Though I had to control myself and not buy too much. That would defeat the purpose of being at the fair to begin with. I was here to make money to help with my bills. There wasn't much left over for extras.

There were so many interesting things I wanted to check out, like the beaded onyx and silver necklaces an older lady made. Then there was the woman who made birthstone rings, and the braided bracelets the young girl across from me made. I intended to get around to all of them at some point.

I walked across the midway, headed toward one of the other booths. My visit wasn't just for the items, though. I wanted to talk to the woman who sold handmade hats. Maybe she had information relevant to the case. She made all different styles and they were absolutely exquisite. Obviously, she had an immense amount of talent.

The woman was waiting on a customer. She wore a cowboy hat with her long, brown hair peeking out from underneath. I assumed she'd made the hat. It was a beautiful natural color with a colored band around the middle.

After a few seconds, she turned her attention to me and smiled. "Let me know if there's anything I can help you with."

There was definitely something she could help me with, but I wasn't quite sure how to start the conversation. After debating for a couple seconds, I decided it was best to ease into it.

"Your hats are beautiful," I said.

"Thank you," she said, flashing her gorgeous smile again. "Would you like to try one on? I know all of them would be fantastic on you."

"Well, that one is nice," I said, pointing to the pale yellow fedora. "I'm amazed at how beautiful they are. It must take a lot of work."

She reached for the hat. "I've been doing it for a while. You'd be surprised how quickly I can make a hat. Not that there isn't a lot of work involved."

"Of course," I said. "I completely understand the time and effort it takes. I have a booth just down the way. I paint."

"Oh, that's fantastic. I'll have to stop by to check out your work before the fair's over."

"That would be nice," I said.

She placed the hat on my head and then pulled out a mirror. "Here you are, take a gander."

"It is a nice hat." As I stared at my reflection, I contemplated how I would broach the subject of murder. It wasn't exactly an easy topic to bring up, not like talking about the weather.

"It would be nice if you stopped by my trailer. Have you been to other vendors' booths?" I asked.

"Um, yes, a few, I suppose," she said as she adjusted the hat back on the stand.

"I don't know the fairground well. You must know your way around here," I said.

Where was I going with this? I had wanted to be smooth with my questioning, but I cringed on the inside at my lack of finesse. It got even worse when I blurted out, "I heard that you were near the trailer on the night of the murder."

I'd overheard Pierce mention this while speaking with another detective. He had no idea I'd heard that part of their conversation.

She focused on her hats. Maybe she wasn't going to answer me. This was kind of awkward. Should I just walk away and give up on this mission? No, I had to press forward. She would talk eventually. I knew based on her body's stance that she wanted to talk. She had something she wanted to get off her chest.

"Yes, I saw something," she said, her voice quiet.

"You saw the person? The killer?"

"I don't know. I saw someone leaving, but I didn't

have a good viewpoint. I've tried to remember, but it just doesn't come to me," she said.

"That's understandable, but I was there too, and I saw someone. I wonder if we saw the same person. Maybe it would spark something in our memories if we talked about it?"

She sighed. "I guess it can't hurt."

I was willing to do anything to unearth a new clue. My desperation was growing by the minute and this felt like my final opportunity. I hoped this conversation might lead to something good.

To encourage her, I said, "I saw someone in an Elvis costume, but he was too far away to see more. Of course, all the Elvis impersonators were wearing the same sort of costumes with the same sort of wigs, so how could I know who was the killer? Did you think that as well?"

"Yes, I did, but just like you, I can't be sure of any details about the person. I don't know for sure if that was the killer."

I felt defeated. There was nothing else I could do, and she had no other memories, just like me. I felt like such a failure.

"Well, if you think of anything else, will you get in touch with me?" I asked.

"Of course I'll let you know."

"I'm in booth number thirty-four by the big tree stump," I added.

Maybe she just wanted to forget altogether and push it out of her mind. Should I purchase the hat? I checked my reflection. My mother always said I was a hat person. I checked the price tag. My sales at the fair would cover it nicely.

"I'll take it," I said.

When I came to the booth of the man who painted artwork similar to mine, I couldn't resist taking a peek at his pieces. One canvas in particular caught my eye and I made a beeline for it. I stood in front of the painting: a beautiful landscape of a farmhouse and a field. Something about the picture drew me to it. It was absolutely stunning and I knew I had to have it. With no price attached, though, I was almost afraid to ask. I spotted the man putting out another painting.

"Hi, sir," I said, capturing his attention. "I'm interested in your painting. Can you tell me the price?"

"That one is forty-five."

I hoped he didn't mean forty-five hundred. I might fall out on the ground right there.

"Forty-five dollars?" I asked.

"Yes," he said with a smile.

That was a price I could handle.

"Sold," I said.

He smiled. "I'll wrap it up for you."

As I waited, I checked out his other items. Soon my attention was pulled away from the art. I spotted someone out of the corner of my eye and I thought he was coming my way. I couldn't believe it was Justin Blackburn. The guy who had warned his girlfriend about speaking to the police.

I'd been searching for him. Though now that I'd found him, I was having second thoughts. I hoped he wasn't coming over to confront me. What if he accused me of spying on him? He couldn't prove it. All he could do was tell me to get lost and leave him alone.

"Here you are, young lady," the artist said, snapping me back to the reason for my visit. He held out the painting, nicely wrapped in brown paper and tied with string.

I didn't want to take my eyes off Justin, though. What if he was planning an attack? I had to be ready for the possibility. I handed the vendor cash, then quickly turned my attention back toward the pathway. Justin was nowhere in sight. Where had he gone? Instantaneously, I panicked.

"The painting." The man gestured.

"Oh yes, sorry," I said, taking the package from him.

With the painting in my arms, I headed down the path toward my trailer. I'd almost made it back when someone called out my name. When I spun around, I spotted Caleb headed my way.

"What you got there?" He pointed.

"Oh, I couldn't help myself, I bought a painting. As if I don't have enough, right?"

He laughed. "Well, if you see something you like, you should go for it."

Caleb held my gaze for a beat before looking away. Was there some hidden meaning in that comment?

"Well, anyway, it's mine," I said.

"Can I see it?" he asked.

I glanced down at the canvas in my hand. "Sure."

"Oh, it's all wrapped up. Maybe I can come by later?" Caleb asked.

"Yeah, I'd like that," I said.

"I can bring Gumshoe and the pups can play." Van loved to romp with Caleb's sweet-natured German shepherd.

"That sounds good," I said. "Oh, by the way, I saw that guy. Justin? I told you about him. Anyway, he was weirding me out. I thought he was coming over to confront me, then the artist handed the painting to me, so I glanced away. When I turned back around, Justin was gone."

Caleb clicked his tongue, "Hmm . . . well, if you see him again, make sure to let me know right away, okay?"

"I promise I will," I said.

"I'll see you around nine o'clock?" he asked.

"Sounds good."

"Nice hat, by the way." Caleb pointed at my head.

I touched the brim. "Oh, thanks, I forgot I was wearing it."

He winked and then walked back across the path in the opposite direction. I was happy we were getting together later because I had a couple of ideas I wanted to check out. I needed to drop off the painting first, though, because I couldn't lug it around while investigating a murder.

The last rays of sunshine faded across the blue horizon and streaks of red and purple blazed across the sky, bringing darkness. I rushed up to the trailer, but before opening the door, I sensed a presence.

I clutched my chest. "Oh, you scared me."

"Well, isn't that what ghosts do?" Donald asked.

"I was just going inside to put this away and then get myself a snack," I said as I reached for the trailer door.

"Peanut butter and banana sandwich?" he asked.

"You really do that all the time, huh?"

"Well, I'm in character," he said. "I'm supposed to do the things Elvis did."

I sighed. "I guess, if you say so."

As soon as I stepped into the trailer, Van jumped up from his bed, wagging his tail as he ran over to me. I picked him up and gave him kisses.

"Are you ready for dinner, Van?" I asked, setting him back on the floor. "I know I am."

"He probably likes peanut butter and banana too," Donald said.

After giving Van his food, I slathered peanut butter on two slices of bread and made a sandwich, minus the banana.

"The only reason I made this sandwich is because you kept talking about peanut butter and I had no bananas." I took off my hat and set it on the counter.

He smiled, as if satisfied with his persuasive skills. "What are you doing?"

"What do you mean?" I asked as I took a bite.

"With the murder investigation. Are you any closer?"

No pressure, no pressure at all. I made a show of chewing my sandwich, mostly to give myself time to think of what to tell him. I was pretending like the peanut butter was stuck to the roof of my mouth.

Finally, when I could stall no longer, I said, "I've been mulling over a few thoughts."

"Such as?" he asked.

"Well, I have a list of suspects."

"Yes?" he said, expecting me to continue.

"And I've been thinking about their motives."

"All right, this sounds promising," he said with a nod. "Can I see that list?"

"It's in my head," I said, tapping my temple with my index finger.

"Maybe you should write it down. That might actually help you think of more," he said. "And maybe I'll recognize a name and it'll spark something."

That wasn't a bad idea. Maybe he was on to something. I put down my sandwich and pushed to my feet.

"Where are you going?" he asked.

"To find a piece of paper," I said.

"You're the best." He pointed.

I grabbed my bag and rooted around in the bottom until I located a scrap piece of paper and a pen. "Found it."

I jotted down the suspects. Justin? His girlfriend Kaye might have information, and as much as I hated it, I needed to track him down. Then there was Dallas, Sammie's date. As I scribbled his name, I was reminded that I needed to call to check on her. Who else was on my list? There had to be more than just those two. What about Donald's fiancée? I'd called her, but she had been unwilling to talk. Unless I traveled to South Carolina to her house, I wouldn't be able to find out more about her. Even then, she probably wouldn't talk to me.

"That's it?" Donald asked as he peeked over my shoulder.

"I'm working on it," I said, stuffing the paper into my bag and out of sight.

Moving on from the list of suspects, I examined the painting I'd finished. The one of the secluded drive down the narrow lane to my cottage tucked among the trees. Even though it appeared complete, there was still something holding me back from placing it outside to sell. Something told me to check out this landscape with the glass. Instructions from my spirit guide? I held the glass jar up to my eye and scanned the canvas. After a few seconds, I spotted the skeleton. The bony figure peered out from the artwork.

"That's odd," I said.

Donald surveyed the artwork. "Maybe it's an omen."

"Does that mean I'm going be murdered soon?" I asked in a wild voice.

"I don't think so," he said. "Take another gander."

"How can you be sure?" I asked.

"Well, I'm not sure, but I wanted to make you feel better."

I sighed. "Thanks for that."

"Check the painting again. Maybe you'll figure out something else." Donald pointed.

The painting was rich in detail, the massive trees full of greenery. How long would it take to search this piece of art? I did as Donald instructed and held the jar up to my eye once again and began my search anew. To my surprise, in the top right-hand corner next to a tree branch, there was another skeleton holding a painting. In my painting, I saw the image of the painting I'd just purchased. How odd was that?

"Maybe the skeleton in this painting depicts someone who's buying a painting from me?"

"Yes, that has to be it," Donald said. "So don't worry."

"Everything's just fine, I suppose," I said.

I put down the jar, though I wasn't completely convinced that I shouldn't panic. I'd had enough of this for the evening, so I decided to tidy up before Caleb arrived. I cleaned up my paints and turned toward where Donald had stood. He was gone.

I moved over to the trailer window to peek outside. I just wanted to make sure there was nothing suspicious going on out there. I wanted to reassure myself that things would be just fine if I relaxed, but the skeletons were still on my mind. Nevertheless, I had to do something to ease my fears. I stared out into the dark night for a while longer. All was quiet, which surprised me because it wasn't even that late.

"Everything is safe out there, Van," I said. "Caleb will be here soon. Gumshoe is coming too."

Van knew the name "Gumshoe" and jumped down from the pillow. He wagged his tail excitedly and danced around in a couple circles. After one last glance, I lowered the blind slat. The uneasiness stayed with me as I paced across the trailer floor. I hoped no one decided to make me the target tonight.

CHAPTER 22

Travel Trailer Tip #22
A good solo activity is journaling. It's a perfect opportunity to jot down clues or lists of suspects.

Reading a few pages of a book while I waited for Caleb, I managed to relax just a bit. That came to an abrupt end when a noise startled me. I fought the urge to jump into bed and hide under the covers. Being a scaredy-cat wasn't the answer. Goose bumps rippled along my skin as I made my way to the door. My heart thumped a little faster as I opened the door and peeked outside. So far, I saw nothing out of the ordinary. Just the empty night.

I had to check outside to make sure my trailer was secure. The last thing I needed was for it to move with Van and me inside. As I walked away from my trailer, I moved toward the corner to see what had made such a racket. Of course, my breathing was almost nonexistent at this point. I was pretty sure I was on the verge of hyperventilating. Nonetheless, I pushed forward. I had to get to the bottom of this.

When I reached the edge of the trailer, I paused and peeked over the side, just in case someone waited there for me. Thank goodness no one was there. Other than the sounds of crickets and katydids, all was quiet and the veil of darkness filled the sky. I scanned around, trying to focus my eyes on the pitch black. No one was there for sure. Well, unless they hid behind the cover of night. I looked down and spotted a shirt. That hadn't been there before.

I picked it up. Where had this come from? Someone had lost their shirt? That meant they had been around my trailer. But why? This was really odd. Chills prickled along my skin. I peered out across the way again, but saw no one. Clutching the shirt, I rushed back toward the trailer door, hurrying inside and closing the door behind me. Van just sat there watching me, as if asking what trouble I'd gotten into this time.

"Van," I said. "Somebody really was messing around out there."

I examined the shirt to see if maybe by some chance a name was on it. Of course, there wasn't. Regardless, the shirt seemed familiar. A graphic design from the band The Rolling Stones was on the front of the T-shirt. I'd seen it before. But where? What was I thinking? These kinds of T-shirts were everywhere. Of course I recognized it. I put the shirt down on the counter and focused on it.

Then it hit me. I remembered where I'd seen that black band shirt. I was almost positive I'd seen Justin Blackburn wearing it in a photo. It had been tacked up on a bulletin board at one of the food vendors. Along with other photos of what I assumed were friends of the booth's owner. I just had to get my hands on that picture one more time to confirm it.

This was a start in the right direction. An Elvis impersonator was the killer. An Elvis impersonator was lurking outside my trailer in the middle of the night, losing, for whatever reason, his shirt. I didn't believe in coincidences—this was all part of the same web.

Then I remembered something else from the photo I'd seen at the booth. He liked to tuck shirts into his waistband. Shirts he wasn't wearing. That meant he probably hadn't been wearing this one at the time he'd been at my trailer. He'd just had it tucked into his waistband. If he'd tucked it behind him, it would look like he had a tail. Kind of like the rat he was. How fitting. I wasn't sure why he did that, or if there was any significance to it. I supposed it didn't matter.

I checked the time on my phone. Was there enough time to hunt down that photo again before Caleb arrived? It wasn't a good idea to search for a killer when it was pitch black out. Darkness would give a killer plenty of places to hide. I didn't want to give a killer the upper hand. Maybe I should wait until the morning. But I really wanted to act on this right away. Would Caleb want to go with me? Likely he'd want to go alone.

I checked my phone again. I'd just have to make enough time to find the photo I'd seen hanging up at one of the junk food vendors. I'd had a weak moment and ordered a fried Oreo. Then I could rush back to my trailer before Caleb arrived. This plan sounded good in my head and I had my fingers crossed that it would actually work that way.

After leaving my trailer, I walked at a brisk pace but didn't quite run. I didn't want to draw attention to myself. The crowd had thinned out on the midway. The rides were winding down and people were finishing playing the games, hoping to win a prize before the end of the night.

Soon I had reached the concession booth. Or, as my mother called it, the sugar coma stand. The smell of fried everything drifted through the air. I hoped not to see the guy so that I could study the photo posted there. I inched closer. With the worker still helping other people, I hoped he wouldn't notice me. What would I say if he saw me? I supposed I'd have to order something. Maybe a corn dog. Did it matter at this point? I just hoped I didn't get nervous and blow my cover. What was I saying? I had no cover. My pretense was buying food. If I didn't get something, that would make him suspicious.

I leaned close to get a good view of the photo. The man was standing next to a stage at another fair. Sure enough, it was him. Justin wore the black Rolling Stones shirt in the photo, with another one tucked into his waistband. It had to have been him at my trailer. This wasn't a coincidence. Why was he around my trailer if he wasn't the killer? That thought sent a shiver down my spine. Just as I was about to move away, I tumbled forward, knocking down bags of buttery popcorn and pink cotton candy from the corner of the stand. That had been a terrible move.

The worker whipped around. With a frown on his face, he asked, "What are you doing?"

I scrambled to pick up the bags and set them back on the counter. "Sorry about that. I was just trying to see the menu. I guess I need glasses."

His brows pinched together. "What can I get for you?"

"Just a corn dog," I said.

A name was printed on his white T-shirt: Barney. Well, Barney was about to unknowingly help me solve a murder investigation. Barney turned away to get my food. Every few seconds, he glanced my way to see what I was up to. I had the information I needed now that I had confirmed Justin was the one who wore T-shirts in his waistband.

What should I do? I had to tell Caleb. Should I ask Barney about the potential killer? If I didn't, it would be a missed opportunity. Though based on the scowl Barney presented, he didn't appear friendly. He might not answer my questions. What was the worst that could happen, though? Barney could tell me to get lost. I expected him to do that anyway. He turned back around and shoved the corn dog at me. I handed over a few crumpled dollars.

When I didn't say anything, Barney eyed me up and down. "Can I get anything else for you?"

I pointed at the photo posted on the bulletin board next to the display of candy apples. Other photos of what I assumed were all friends of the men working the booth were pinned to the board as well.

"I saw the picture and I couldn't help but notice the guy. I think I know him. Is he around here? Does he work here?"

Barney lifted an eyebrow. "Yeah, Justin's around somewhere. Can I tell him who asked?"

No way would I provide my real name. It was bad enough Barney would be able to identify me by sight.

"I'm a friend of a friend. Mary is my friend. My name's Laura."

I'd made that up out of thin air. Where did I come up

with this stuff? Maybe I'd watched too many episodes of *Little House on the Prairie*. Or, as I used to call it when I was little and had missing front teeth, *Little House on the Fairy*.

Barney said, "Yeah, I'll tell him."

"How do you know Justin? Is he a nice guy?"

Barney wiped his hands on a towel that didn't look much cleaner than his hands. He eyed me suspiciously. "If you know him, wouldn't you know he's a nice guy?"

Yes, I supposed that was a valid question. Based on Barney's comment, I figured I had my answer. Barney didn't seem friendly and I was almost certain Justin had the same irritated disposition.

By the time Barney relayed the message, I'd be long gone. At least, that was my plan. I hurried away before he caught on to my fibs. As I pulled out my phone to text Caleb, I glanced over my shoulder. Barney still watched me. Maybe he knew more about Justin than he let on and was surprised I'd actually asked about him. Maybe Barney knew that Justin had killed Donald.

Calling was out of the question; the noise of the rides made it impossible to hear. Instead, I feverishly typed out a message to Caleb: **Someone was messing around my trailer.**

I probably sounded paranoid, but this time I had some proof to show that someone had been there. When Caleb didn't respond right away, I continued. **I think the killer lost his shirt at my trailer.**

Okay, that sounded ridiculous. Perhaps I needed to elaborate. **I think I know who the shirt belongs to . . .**

I hoped Caleb didn't think I was too nuts. I hurried down the midway with my corn dog and the smell of fried food lingering in the air.

Seconds later, Caleb responded: **Where are you?**

On the midway. Going back to my trailer, I typed back.

I'll meet you there.

I just hoped Caleb wanted to see the shirt. Then I could bring him back to the food stand and show him the photo. That might be all he needed to make an arrest. Wouldn't it be nice if we got this wrapped up tonight? I hurried my pace because it felt as if someone was watching me. I hoped I was just paranoid, thinking that Justin had been at my trailer. Nevertheless, I didn't want to take any chances.

"Are you making progress?" a male voice said from beside me.

I jumped and clutched my chest. "Oh, it's you. Where have you been?"

"I'm not sure. In between worlds, I guess you could say," Donald said

I wouldn't know because I wasn't sure how this whole paranormal thing worked.

"Are you all right?" I asked.

"Absolutely," he said.

I scanned the area to see if anyone was watching me talk to myself.

"We'd better get to my trailer," I said out of the corner of my mouth. "I'm expecting company anyway."

"Right," Donald said as he followed along beside me.

I stood in front of my tiny trailer, waiting for Caleb. A strange energy surrounded me and I was farther away from any of the activity, which made things even scarier. Other people had turned in for the evening, apparently, because a lot of lights were off. A few people mingled down the way. They weren't close enough for my liking. I was standing out here all by myself.

"Maybe I should just wait inside," I said. "I don't like hanging out here alone."

Donald said, "You're not alone. I'm here with you. There's nothing to be worried about."

"No offense, I can see you, but no one else can. For all they know, I'm out here alone."

"Yes, but if someone came along, I could help you."

"By doing what? Saying 'boo?' " I asked.

"Well, now you're just stereotyping," he said.

"Sorry," I said. "I'm just a little stressed."

"It's understandable, but if someone comes along, I really could help. Like you said, I could scare them, or maybe I can use enough energy to throw something at them."

I gave him a faint smile. "That's very sweet of you to offer."

"Hey, that's what friends are for," he said.

An owl hooted from a nearby tree and I jumped.

"You're really jittery tonight," he said.

"Maybe I should text Caleb again to ask if he's on his way yet."

"You don't want to seem too needy," Donald said with a wink.

"I am needy! I'm in need of not getting murdered!"

"Fair point."

I paced in front of the trailer, sending Caleb another text and anxiously waiting for a reply.

"You're making me nervous," he said.

"This is the only way I can calm myself down. I have to keep busy."

A rustling noise came from over my shoulder and I spun around, thrusting my hands forward as if I was ready to punch whoever might be there.

"Who is that?" I asked.

It was unlikely anyone would answer, especially if it was the killer. No one was there and I was almost too afraid to investigate.

"Perhaps it's time for me to go inside and wait," I whispered.

"Well, you should have thought of that earlier," a deep, familiar voice said from over my shoulder.

I spun around to find Caleb in front of me.

"Oh, you're here," I said, clutching my chest. "Thank goodness."

"Is everything okay?" Caleb asked.

"I thought I heard a noise, but obviously it was nothing. I want to tell you about this shirt I found behind my trailer. I think someone was here. If you come back to the food stand with me, I can show you a picture of the guy. We have to go find him. I think he's the killer."

"I believe you," Caleb said. "But just because you found the shirt doesn't mean he's the killer. He could just have been walking in the area. I can talk to him, though, and ask."

"He won't admit it," I said.

"No, but I'm a good judge of people. I'll know if he's lying."

"You know if someone is lying?" I asked.

The side of his mouth lifted in a small grin. "Yes, I'm good at knowing if someone is fibbing to me. Such as when they say they aren't investigating a crime they've been told not to."

He had me there.

"So I did all this for nothing," I said.

"Detective work is hard, Celeste. It's takes a long time, and sometimes you never see the reward," Caleb said.

"I don't like to take no for an answer," I said.

"Don't I know that," Caleb said.

"Sounds like you're a real handful," Donald piped in.

"Is something else wrong?" Caleb asked, noticing when I shot Donald a glare.

I had to tell him about the ghost. I exhaled. "Here's the thing . . . the ghost of the murdered man is here," I said.

Caleb surveyed the area. "A ghost is here?"

Thank goodness I'd already told Caleb about my ability to see ghosts. It was nice having someone to share this craziness with, and that he didn't freak out about it either.

"I doubt you'll see him."

"Well, if he's here, why can't he just tell you who killed him?" Caleb asked.

"He doesn't remember."

Caleb groaned. "Of course he doesn't."

"Hey, I'm trying," Donald said, forgetting Caleb couldn't hear him. "You try recalling the details of your own murder!"

I didn't want to make Donald feel worse than he already did. "He's trying to remember, but so far, it's been spotty," I said.

"That's understandable, I suppose," Caleb said.

At least Caleb didn't think I was crazy for what I'd just told him.

"Is there anything we can do to help him remember?" Caleb asked.

"I haven't figured that out yet," I said.

"Maybe if we re-created the crime scene it would spark something," Donald said.

I turned to Donald, eyebrows raised. Now that wasn't a bad idea.

"What did he say?" Caleb asked.

"He wants to re-create the crime scene," I said.

"Even with the jelly doughnut," Donald added.

"Jelly doughnut and all." I grimaced when I realized how ridiculous this all sounded.

"Well, you can tell the ghost," Caleb peered around, as if searching for Donald, "the trailer is gone, so we can't re-create the scene."

"We can use Celeste's trailer," Donald offered optimistically.

"Apparently," I said, "we can just use mine."

Chapter 23

Travel Trailer Tip #23
Charades is another entertaining game. There are so many fun ways to act out murder clues.

We spent the rest of the evening re-creating the crime scene. I laid Caleb down on the floor, just as I had seen Donald. I didn't have any wire or doughnuts, so we made do with some yarn I had lying around and a bagel.

"I still think we should go out and get the doughnut," Donald said, his eyes wistful. "For the full effect."

"The shop is closed," I said, placing the bagel in Caleb's sprawled-out hand. "Now, watch me fake-choke Caleb."

Despite our impressive performances, it didn't spark anything in Donald, except perhaps a dash of residual trauma. Soon, Caleb left, Donald disappeared, and I was alone in my trailer once again. I put the painting of the old farmhouse and the field full of bright red wildflowers on the counter, propped up against the wall. I studied it for quite a while. What was it about this painting? Why had my painting instructed me to buy it? I assumed that was why I'd been so drawn to it and compelled to buy it. The hidden image within my painting had shown me a skeleton purchasing a painting. I knew it was that painting.

Nothing seemed out of the ordinary. There was nothing particularly special about the artwork. I picked up the jar and held it up to my eye. Maybe there was a hidden image within this painting too. Did the artist have the same psychic talent I did? I studied every inch of it, but there was nothing hidden.

I put down the glass jar. "Well, that rules out that theory, Van."

He barked in agreement. With my hands on my hips, I studied the canvas a bit longer. Still, nothing came to me. I guessed I should give up on trying to figure this out for the night. Had my psychic painting actually subconsciously told me to buy this one? It just made no sense.

I sighed and picked up the canvas, placing it down on the floor for safekeeping. Maybe I would never know the reason. Perhaps the psychic talent guiding me thought I should have it for its beauty alone.

When I turned around to get my pajamas, a crashing noise echoed through the trailer. I spun around to find Van had jumped up onto the counter and knocked over a bottle of solvent.

"Oh no, Van, what are you doing?"

He hurried down and jumped over to his bed. I wasn't sure if he wanted to get away from the disaster or was just pretending he had no hand in this accident. But instead of looking remorseful, he seemed oddly pleased with himself.

Solvent had dripped all over the beautiful painting. I moved closer to the canvas to examine the damage. The solvent had dissolved the paint. Another image appeared underneath. Of course it had been damaged by the solvent too, but not as much, and I was still able to make out the scene. Perhaps the artist had reused the canvas. The top painting was definitely ruined. I picked up a rag and wiped off the paint.

Enough of the top paint had been removed to reveal what was under it. It appeared to be a full painting, not just the start of one. I'd reused canvases before, but never one that I actually sold. I wiped off more of the paint. It was stunning. A sweeping view of the chateau of Chambord, among the backdrop of oak, chestnut, and birch trees. Towers rose up toward the azure sky, and the same hue colored the water of the moat. The underlying painting was much better than the one I had originally purchased. Why would he paint over something so beautiful?

I thought I recognized the artwork. It was the one that had been stolen, the case Pierce was on. At least I was almost positive it was. I'd have to confirm it with him. Or maybe an expert the department had hired. It had been here, right under our noses all along. It had taken Van and his extraspecial skills to uncover the truth. That pup! He always knew.

I pulled out my phone and dialed Pierce. Unfortunately, he didn't answer, so I had to leave a message. I hoped he would get back to me soon. I had to secure the painting so that no one would see it or have access to it. Having it locked away in my trailer would have to be good enough.

CHAPTER 24

Travel Trailer Tip #24
Picking a spot near the woods to park your travel trailer isn't always a good idea. Be alert for anyone who might be hiding in the trees.

After driving a short distance from the fairgrounds, I parked my pink trunk outside the Sevier County theater. A large, flashing sign guided people toward the area where the celebrity impersonator concert would be held tonight. I wished I'd gotten here earlier so I could talk to someone. But I'd only found out about this at the last minute, so I would have to make the most of the situation.

I climbed out of the truck and hurried across the parking lot, on high alert to see if anyone had followed me. So far, there was no sign of anything suspicious. I quickened my step and reached the ticket booth.

"One, please," I said.

Having someone with me would have been nice, but

there was no time to wait for anyone to arrive. The middle-aged woman behind the glass partition handed me a ticket after I handed her the cash.

"Have a good time," she said without peering up at me.

"Thanks," I said.

She didn't respond. I hurried to the door but stopped before walking in so I could get my bearings and figure out where I needed to go next. I assumed anyone I might need to speak with would be behind the stage. I opened the door and stepped inside the air-conditioned building. Ushers and people attending the concert moved about, but they wouldn't have the information I needed.

I glanced around and spotted a door marked *Private* and assumed it led backstage. It was probably locked. There had to be a way to sneak in, though. I wouldn't let something as simple as a locked door stand in the way of my solving this case. After glancing around again and making sure no one was paying attention to me, I walked over to the door.

When I twisted the knob, it opened. Wow, could it really be that easy? I opened it and then peeked inside. Sure enough, the long hallway led to the back of the stage. People dressed in shiny costumes moved around with guitars slung over their shoulders.

Going unnoticed, I stepped down the hallway and headed toward the stage. When I reached the back area, I looked for anyone who might be able to guide me in the right direction. I hoped no one realized I wasn't supposed to be back here.

I spotted a man with a clipboard. Though I figured he might ask me to leave. When I noticed a young couple dressed in matching gold-and-white costumes, I decided to approach them instead. Unfortunately, I only made it a couple of steps toward them when someone yelled out, "Hey, you're not supposed to be back here."

Oh no. I'd been caught.

When I peeked back, I spotted the man with the clipboard staring at me. I moved to my right into a darkened area. I hoped I wouldn't trip over something. The man would probably come after me or call Security. Or both.

My eyes adjusted to the dark room. Lights and props for the stage filled the space as I maneuvered around them. I had no idea where I was headed. I just wanted to get out of this place. Maybe I'd have to abandon the whole mission of finding more information about who might want Donald dead. Could I wait outside for the show to end and then find somebody to talk to me? That might be safer than hiding out in here.

I had to focus on one problem at a time. An angry employee was searching for me, and he might have called the police. What would Caleb and Pierce say about this little snafu? Yeah, I already knew they wouldn't like it.

A rustling sounded from nearby and I assumed it wasn't a mouse. Unless it was a very big rat wearing jeans and a Polo shirt. I hid behind a large wooden prop designed to look like a tree full of green leaves and held my breath, hoping the man wouldn't find me.

After a few seconds, the footsteps stopped. I didn't dare peek around the wooden prop for fear the man would be waiting right there for me. The footsteps started again. How long would I have to wait to make sure he'd gone?

Releasing a lungful of air, I peered around the edge of the prop. No sign of the man. I eased out and across the space again. What would I do once I reached the hallway again? My anxiety spiked at the thought of peering out into the corridor. Staying back here for much longer wasn't an option.

When I reached the edge of the room, I mustered my courage and peered around the side. It appeared as if the coast was clear. The man with the clipboard was gone, but I needed to hurry to make this a productive trip before it was too late.

Heading out down the hallway, I searched for someone who might talk to me. A burly guy stood in the corner by the stage entrance. We made eye contact and he seemed friendly enough, so I approached him.

"How can I help you, little lady?" he asked.

Before I had a chance to ask anything, I noticed someone else I recognized. Justin Blackburn. The man noticed me eyeing Justin. The one who had lost his shirt behind my trailer.

"Do you know him?" he asked.

"As a matter of fact, yes. Do you know him?" I asked.

"He's a performer here, so yeah, I know him. Is he a friend of yours?"

"Not exactly," I said.

"Yeah, you seem too nice to have a friend as snotty as him."

"Oh really? He's not friendly to you?" I asked

"No, but he should be. I'm the one who got him the gig here. I don't care how good he is, he's not coming back for the next event."

Wow, what had Justin done to make this man so angry? I had to find out. "What did he do?" I pressed.

The man scoffed. "What hasn't he done? He just has a

bad attitude in general. From the first moment he came in here. He thought he should have all the special perks, but that wasn't going to happen."

"Interesting," I said.

The man frowned. "And who are you again?"

I hadn't told him who I was, and I wondered if I should. I supposed there was no harm in that.

"My name's Celeste Cabot. I'm a painter with a booth at the county fair. That's how I know Justin. He's performing there too."

"I hope he isn't creating as much havoc there as he is here."

Apparently. this guy had no idea about the murder.

"Well, there's a lot going on at the fair this year," I said.

"Yes, I heard about that. I knew Donald."

"Really?" I asked. "Do you know why someone would want to kill him?"

"I can't think of anything. Donald was a nice guy. He'd give you the shirt off his back."

"That's true, I would have," Donald said from over my shoulder. "Too bad I can't remember anything about this guy. Being a ghost is tough."

"Do you think Justin could have anything to do with Donald's murder?" I asked. There was no easy way to just come out and ask that question.

The man glanced toward the stage. "I suppose I hadn't thought about it, but now that you've asked, I guess there is a chance. We never really know anyone, do we?"

"No, we don't. If there's anything else you think of, will you contact me?" I handed him my card.

My artwork covered the front of my cards. I'd decided on the painting of the sunset glow over the Great Smoky

Mountains in hues of auburn, gold, and crimson. Wispy fog topped the silhouettes of the mountaintops on a picture-perfect fall morning.

He studied it and then nodded. "Yes, I'll definitely call you."

"Thank you," I said.

Out of the corner of my eye, something moved. When I peered down the hall, I noticed the worker with the clipboard who had come after me.

"Okay, well, is there another way to get out of here?" I asked.

"The door down there." He pointed.

Right in the direction from which I had come and where the worker was on the hunt. I'd just have to deal with him if I went down the hall. I had no other choice. I'd march right past him and ignore him. What could he do to me? I was leaving anyway.

"Thanks again," I said.

"No problem."

I turned around and headed down the hallway.

The man with the clipboard yelled out, "Hey, you, come here. I want to talk to you. What are you doing? You can't be back here."

"Oh I can't? I'm sorry about that. I'll be leaving now," I said in an innocent voice.

He frowned as I hurried past.

"You should see the look on his face," Donald said with a laugh. "I never did like that guy. Oh, hey, I remembered something about him."

"That's fantastic, Donald. What can you tell me about him?"

"Well, he . . . um, yeah, I guess all I remember is that I didn't like him."

"Oh, that's disappointing. Though I suppose it's a start."

"I should do something to prank him."

"Let's just get out of here. You don't need to do anything at all," I said.

"Did you say something?" the man asked.

He'd thought I was talking to him.

"No, I didn't," I said.

"Sure thing, crazy lady," he said with a smirk.

"That was really mean," I said.

"I told you he wasn't nice," Donald said.

"Okay, go ahead and do that prank," I said.

Donald smiled. "Gladly. Watch this."

Chapter 25

Travel Trailer Tip #25
Taking in local events can be a great way to connect with the local grapevine—always a good source of clues.

Donald ran in front of the man and knocked over one of the lights. It landed right in the man's path. He jumped back, clearly startled. Donald was obviously learning how to use his ghostly skills.

"What in the heck?" he asked. He turned around and stared at me as if I'd had something to do with it.

"Hmm, now that was certainly crazy," I said with a smug expression, enjoying his gaping face.

I continued toward the exit, a strut in my step. That had totally freaked him out. I opened the door and walked into the lobby, thankful to be in the light again.

Donald appeared next to me. "What do you make of that visit?" he asked as I headed for the exit.

"Disappointing, for sure. All I really learned is that Justin isn't a nice guy. I already knew that. I hope it leads to something. I'd hate to think I made this trip for nothing."

"You certainly are a good detective," Donald said.

I stepped through the door. "Thank you. I can always use a compliment. Caleb and Pierce obviously never want me to do anything like this."

"I appreciate that you're trying to help me," he said.

"Of course, Donald," I replied, giving him a sad smile.

He held my gaze, and I thought I could see ghostly tears forming in his eyes. But as soon as I noticed, he cleared his throat. "So where to?" he asked.

"I guess I'll just go back to my trailer and think on it for a bit. There has to be something else I can do. I hate wasting time and not having something planned."

"You certainly like to stay active, that's for sure. Why not stay for the show? You bought a ticket."

"Now that I think about it, I should do something else to try to solve this case. Since when do I give up this easily?"

"Perhaps you could go back and visit Madame Gerard again," he said.

"I don't think she would appreciate me visiting after business hours."

"Maybe tomorrow?"

"Yes, maybe tomorrow," I said.

I'd told him that, but I wasn't quite convinced I needed to make that trip. I'd just wait and see what happened. I hopped into the truck. Donald slipped through the passenger door. Pulling away from the curb, I headed back in the direction of the county fair. Another car leaving at the same time was going in the same direction. As I traveled through a traffic light, I glanced in the rearview mirror and noticed the car was still behind me. My chest became tight with a mounting dread.

"Do you see that car back there?" I asked.

Donald turned around and checked. "The red one?"

"Yes. I think it's following me."

"What makes you think that?" he asked.

"Well, it pulled out right at the same time I pulled away from the curb back there. That can't be a coincidence, right?"

"Perhaps it is," he said. "I wouldn't worry about it too much just yet."

If not now, when? I made a quick right turn without giving a signal. When I checked in the mirror, the red car was following me onto this street too.

I swallowed harshly and tried to reach out for my phone while keeping my eyes on the road. But my purse had fallen onto the floor during my sharp turn and I couldn't get to it. Reaching for it would be dangerous. And if I pulled over, I worried that this person would come after me.

"Donald . . . do you think you could hand me my phone from my purse?"

It took him a few tries, his hands running right through it until—finally—he was able to get a firm grasp,

"Oh, Celeste," he said, his voice quaking. "You aren't going to like this."

"What? What is it?"

"There's no service."

Of course there wasn't! Why would there be while I was being chased down on an empty road? I glanced at my mirror again. The red car was close on my tail.

"What are you going to do?" Donald asked.

"I don't know. This is a tricky situation. What do you think I should do?" I asked. I was ready for any kind of advice I could get.

"Well, I suppose it would be best if you could get away from them rather than just drive around with them following you all the time."

"Obviously, but how am I going to do that?" I asked.

"Good question," he said.

Up ahead, I spotted a building that I knew had an alleyway beside it. This was my chance to turn and possibly lose this car. Though it could be risky if they followed me into the alley. It was a chance I'd have to take. I wasn't sure when I'd get another one to lose my pursuer on this straight-through country road.

As I neared the turnoff, I peered into the rearview mirror. The car hadn't made it to the turn yet, so I had just a few seconds to veer into that alleyway. They'd never know I'd turned down there. It would appear as if I'd just disappeared right off the street. I'd like to see the driver's expression when he realized I was nowhere in sight.

I turned down that alleyway and eased to the back of the building. Then I pulled behind a dumpster.

"What do we do?" Donald asked

"Hope they don't come down here for me. It has to be the killer. Is it just me or is it getting a bit hard to breathe?"

"I'm not the best person to ask, seeing as I'm, you know, dead."

"Right," I said, my voice wavering and my breaths short. "Sorry."

"Try to take deep breaths," Donald said.

I inhaled and released the air from my lungs. "That didn't help. I need to get out of the truck and peek around the side of the dumpster to see if anyone is coming this way."

"Just be careful," Donald said.

He didn't need to tell me to be careful, I knew that all too well. I hopped out of the truck and straight over to the dumpster. I peered around the side. Thank goodness there was no sign of the vehicle. I hoped it stayed that way, but how long would I have to stay back here just to be safe? I stood by the trash container for another minute, watching for any sign of the car, but nothing happened. It was time to get out of there. I hurried back over to the truck.

"What happened?" Donald asked.

I was kind of surprised that he hadn't come out of the truck and followed me over there. Actually, while I was on that train of thought, why didn't he go out there to keep a lookout instead of me? He was already dead! I was about to say that, but it didn't feel very nice or useful now that I was safely back in the truck.

"Well, I think we can get out of here. I didn't see anything. I guess I lost them after all." I felt a rush of pride. "My driving skills are pretty good, huh?"

"Yes, you're an excellent driver," Donald said, rolling his eyes. "Now let's get out of here."

I pulled back out onto the road with no sign of the red car. Thank goodness. I just needed to get back to the fairgrounds before something else crazy happened.

CHAPTER 26

Travel Trailer Tip #26
Going out for a nighttime stroll? It's probably a good idea to invite a friend along. Or a very protective dog.

When I reached the edge of the fairgrounds, my phone alerted me to a text message. **Meet me at the fun house**.

Sammie wanted me to go to the fun house? What was she up to? Didn't she know I was trying to solve the murder? I had little time for fun houses. Nevertheless, I was already here, and well, I couldn't tell her no. Therefore, I headed in the direction of the fun house. I'd never liked those places, and after my recent experience while looking for Kaye, I liked them even less now. They were always kind of creepy, with all the mirrors, clowns, and creepy laughing noises they piped into that confined space. Just the thought brought anxiety as a flashback of recently being in that terror-filled Wacky Shack.

Darkness had settled over town, but the lights from the fairgrounds still lit up the sky. The crowds were thinning out as everyone left to go home for the night. I kept glancing over my shoulder, as if I felt someone behind me. I figured it was just my nerves. Nonetheless, I couldn't get myself to settle down.

The blinking lights of the fun house came into view, but there was no sign of Sammie waiting outside for me. I typed out a text message: **I'm here. Where are you?**

I sent the message and waited, standing in front of the fun house. Flashing light bulbs surrounded the multicolored Fun House sign. The bored attendant didn't bother glancing my way. Had Sammie already gone inside? Should I buy a ticket?

Just then, another text message came through. **I went in without you. Come inside.**

I had to enter this place again? This was just a bit more than I wanted to handle tonight. But I always did what my best friend wanted, so I marched over to the less-than-enthusiastic attendant, handed him the cash, and he thrust the ticket at me. Apparently, he was uninterested in customer service skills. This seemed like déjà vu. I shoved the ticket stub into my pocket in case anyone questioned whether I should be in there and then stepped up the narrow ramp to enter. I couldn't believe I was doing this again.

Upon entering, the floor heaved and moved under my feet, going in odd directions. I used all the muscles in my legs, trying to stand upright to make my way into a different section. Of course, the creepy laughter surrounded me again, coming from all directions. Dark prevailed except for the flashing lights. I found it hard to see my hand in front of my face. Sammie owed me one for this.

Just when I made it through the first obstacle, I was faced with another disaster: spinning discs I was supposed to walk across to get to the other side. How was I supposed to do that without falling to my death? The pictures of the giant clowns on the walls didn't help matters either. When the lights flashed, the wicked smiles were visible. My anxiety grew with each passing second. I was deep into this place now, with still no sign of Sammie. Plus, I couldn't text her because I couldn't even see to type on my phone, much less be able to keep my balance and not drop the phone.

The narrow hallways felt as if they were closing in on me. Maybe I was having a panic attack. I had to get out of this place. Suddenly, it felt as if someone was behind me, just as it had felt when I was walking across the midway. When I glanced back, I caught a glimpse of a silhouette of someone. So, someone was back there after all. It hadn't been my imagination. I didn't know if the person was coming after me, but I wasn't going to take any chances.

I sped up, trying to get through this disaster. The demented recorded clown laughter blasted from the speakers, growing louder with each passing second. I glanced back and realized the person was closing in on me. If I screamed, would anyone hear me? Was Sammie playing a trick on me? Would she jump out at me like the time we'd gone to that haunted house? I still hadn't gotten her back for that. It had taken years off my life.

Finally, the exit came into view. At least, I hoped it was the exit. Just as I reached the doorway, though, my shirt caught on something. I glanced back and saw that the person was gaining on me. With the darkness, I still couldn't make out any features. I frantically pulled on my shirt.

I was in a complete panic by this point. What would I do if I couldn't break free? Could I just strip off the shirt?

No, that was impossible. Panic had me in a tight grip now. This was life-and-death for me. At least, it was in my mind.

With one more big yank, I broke free. I'd ripped my shirt, but I didn't care. I was free and that was all that mattered. Where was Sammie? Why had she left me in there? As I raced from the fun house, I sprinted around the side of the small building and made my way to the midway again. So far, no one was behind me. It appeared that the person who had been in the fun house hadn't followed me. Had that been Sammie?

Mostly everyone had gone home by now. Lights on the rides, games, and vendors were being shut off. Darkness crept in. It was time for me to get to my trailer. As I hurried away from the fun house, I typed out a message to Sammie. **Where are you? Why weren't you at the fun house**?

A text from Sammie came through. **Why would I be at the fun house?**

That was odd. The text asking me to meet her at the fun house had now disappeared. I knew I'd seen it. **I got a text from you asking to meet at the fun house.**

What? I didn't text you. Why would I be there?

This sent a shiver down my spine. Also, it reinforced my thought that I wanted to be in the safety of my trailer. **I definitely received a text**.

Where are you now?

Headed for my trailer.

This is scary, Celeste. You know there are apps that let people manipulate numbers. Text me and let me know when you're safe.

I promise I will.

Everyone had gone home and I was running down the

midway, trying to reach my trailer and the safety of my little space.

When I glanced over my shoulder, I noticed someone following me in the distance. I knew I wouldn't have time to get to my trailer safely before the person reached me. I had to hide. But where? I glanced around, and then I spotted the merry-go-round. That would have to do.

I climbed up onto the platform and found the largest horse to hide behind. The ride was unlit, so I hoped the darkness would conceal me. Nevertheless, I was scared. My heart beat fast as I stood behind the big horse. How long would I have to wait until the coast was clear and I could get to my trailer?

Without warning, the lights on the merry-go-round lit up. Music played and the platform started moving round and round. I clung to the horse, but there was no way I could hide like this for much longer, not with the bright lights. The music pounded in my ears. It was meant to be whimsical, but now it seemed almost sinister. The person who had been following me had to be the one who'd turned on the ride. What a cruel trick to play.

I considered taking my chances and jumping off, but then the merry-go-round sped up even faster. It might be too dangerous to hop off now. How fast could this thing go anyway? I peeked out from around the side of the horse, but I didn't see anyone watching me. They were probably hiding and getting a lot of glee out of this whole thing.

I played through different scenarios in my mind, trying to decide which one was the best option. None of them were any good; nevertheless, I had to make a decision pretty soon. But then, all of a sudden, everything stopped.

The merry-go-round quit moving. The lights went off. The music ended.

I had to get off the ride before it started again. Mustering up all my courage, I dashed around the large horse and moved to the edge. I jumped off without even checking to see if anybody stood nearby.

The night surrounded me. This part of the fairgrounds was on the outer edge, so no one else was around, other than the potential killer, of course. He was playing with me like a cat teasing a mouse before it went in for the kill. When my feet hit the ground, I took off running as fast as my legs would take me. I glanced over my shoulder but saw no one back there.

“Celeste, what are you doing?” someone called out.

Out of the corner of my eye, I spotted Caleb. I stopped and tried to catch my breath as he approached.

“Someone was following me,” I panted.

“What are you doing out here?”

“Never mind that. We need to focus on the fact that someone was back there following me. They turned on the merry-go-round while I was hiding,” I said.

Caleb peered around. “I don’t see anyone.”

“Well, yeah, I guess they left when I jumped off the ride. Somehow, they turned the thing on.”

“Don’t worry. That’s all over,” he said. “Maybe you should go back to your house for the night. I can drive you.”

No, I wasn’t going to agree to that. I was seeing this through. Yes, I was stubborn, but this was important to me.

“I’m staying, Caleb,” I said.

We headed back toward the trailer. I glanced over my shoulder a few times, still feeling a bit paranoid.

"It's okay, Celeste," he said.

At least he wasn't still reminding me about how dangerous this was, and I was thankful for that. When my trailer came into sight, I pulled out my key and unlocked the door. I just wanted to go to bed and try to forget this evening.

"Would you like something to drink?" I asked, gesturing over my shoulder.

"Sure, that would be great. Do you have any of that great lemonade?" he asked.

"I always have lemonade," I said around a laugh.

"You're a great hostess," he said with a wink.

I poured the lemony liquid into a pink plastic tumbler. "Here you are."

"Always pink, huh?" Caleb asked before taking a sip.

"It's my signature color." I took a sip of lemonade.

Caleb set the tumbler down. "Tell me who's on your suspect list."

I studied the floor, avoiding eye contact. "What makes you think I have a list?"

Caleb gave me a look.

When I couldn't handle the silence any longer, I peered up. "Okay, fine, here's my list . . ."

"I'm all ears," Caleb said.

"Justin Blackburn, his girlfriend Kaye, and Dallas." I lowered my voice in case Donald was listening. "Oh, and you might want to check Donald's fiancée, just to be safe."

Caleb leaned back and stretched his arms over his head. "That is certainly an interesting list."

"You're not mad at me?" I asked.

Caleb stood. "Come on, I want to take you somewhere."

I frowned. "It's late. Where are we going?"

He took me by the hand. "You'll find out."

After saying goodbye to Van, Caleb and I stepped out into the night air. A full moon shone and stars twinkled in the velvety sky.

As I slid into Caleb's truck, I asked, "Where are you taking me?"

"It's a surprise," he said. "It won't be a surprise if I tell you."

Should I mention that I don't like surprises? I'm just not capable of handling the suspense. At least he hadn't made me wear a blindfold.

"Okay, close your eyes," he said.

"No way," I said.

"All right, you don't have to close your eyes, but don't pay too much attention, okay? Maybe stare down at your feet." He laughed, but I figured he was only half joking.

"I bet I can guess where we're going," I said after only a couple of minutes.

"Oh, you think you can, huh?" he said.

"As a matter of fact, I would almost guarantee it."

"You know me too well," he said as he pulled the truck into my Aunt Patsy's Paradise Café. "I made a call and she agreed to stay open late just for us."

It had been a while since I'd been here, and I knew my aunt wouldn't be pleased about that. Surely I'd get a scolding once I stepped through the door.

"She's only doing that because she likes you," I said.

"It's been too long since we've had a burger," Caleb said as he shut off the truck.

"I can't deny that," I said.

After Caleb got out from behind the wheel, he hurried around to meet me. We walked up to the door and he opened it for me. A combined smell of baked bread and greasy hamburgers hit us as we stepped through the door.

"My mouth's watering already," Caleb said.

Aunt Patsy spun around with the spatula in her hand raised toward the ceiling.

She lifted a perfectly sculpted eyebrow. "Well, look what the cat dragged in."

"I think we're in trouble," Caleb whispered.

"You have no idea," I said.

Caleb and I cautiously approached the booth we always sat in. We had first shared a meal together at the first booth on the right, close to the front door. I supposed you could say it had been our first date.

Aunt Patsy stomped over to us. "Care to explain what took you so long to get here?"

I opened my mouth to speak, but nothing came out. I had no explanation.

"Celeste and I have been extremely busy with artwork." Caleb stumbled over his words.

"No excuse," Aunt Patsy said, crossing her arms in front of her waist.

"Well, at least we're here now," I said with a grimace.

She eyed me. "Yes, I guess there is that. But don't let it happen again. I'll go get your burgers going. I'll be right back."

"That went better than I thought," I said, as we went to take a seat.

Aunt Patsy had set up her own booth at the fair. She was selling her famous burgers. The ones Caleb claimed were addictive. I couldn't blame him for feeling that way because they were delicious. Aunt Patsy had other good treats at the booth as well, like red velvet cinnamon rolls and Key lime mini pies. The mini pies were a new recipe and I couldn't wait to try them. No doubt they'd be fantastic because everything she made was delightful. Maybe I would try them tomorrow.

"Van is going to be sad he missed this," I said.

"Gumshoe too," Caleb said with a chuckle. "He'll guilt me into giving him another treat to make up for it."

I laughed. "After he detects that we've had late-night snacks."

"You're right about that. No doubt he'll sniff it on us," he said with a laugh.

My mouth watered as I thought about the burgers. When I took Caleb to Aunt Patsy's diner, I had unknowingly created a burger-obsessed monster.

A short time later, Aunt Patsy brought over our burgers. I couldn't believe I was eating greasy food this late at night. Caleb and I always got cheeseburgers and fries. I liked mine cooked extremely well done.

"I thought y'all would never come back." Her cute Southern accent carried across the room. "Even at the fair, I didn't see hide nor hair of either one of you." Her voice dropped off, her face troubled.

"Is everything all right?" I asked.

"I saw something a bit strange at the fair earlier," she said with a worried twist of her mouth. "I had forgotten."

"What was it, Patsy?" Caleb asked.

"Well, maybe it's nothing," she said with the wave of her hand.

"It could be important. You should tell us," he added.

"Well, I saw a man snooping around the booth that sells the paintings. It's the one by the funnel cake stand. A heavyset guy is the artist," she said. "I just thought it seemed odd. The way he was walking around just didn't seem normal."

It couldn't be a coincidence that the booth she described was where I'd purchased the painting. Why hadn't Pierce answered my message about it? Had he even gotten the message? I was anxious to get the thing off my hands.

"Can you describe him?" Caleb asked.

"He had dark, short hair." Patsy gestured at the top of her head. "About your height and weight, Caleb."

"Is there anything else that stands out about him?" I asked.

Patsy grabbed the spatula to flip the burgers on the grill. "I can't think of anything. You can guarantee if I see him again, though, that I'll find out what he's up to."

CHAPTER 27

Travel Trailer Tip #27
Taking nature photography is a great pastime. It can also provide an excuse to get close to a crime scene.

The next day, while I waited for Pierce to arrive to see the painting, I walked up to the stage and peered around. A few people milled around in the distance. I needed to talk with someone—in particular, anyone who could give me information about the area and who might have access to the equipment. Movement came from my right. A tall, dark-haired man wearing a dark T-shirt and jeans was rolling up cable. I headed in his direction. Halfway there, he spotted me. When I smiled, he returned the friendly look.

"What can I do for you?" he asked.

"I'm sorry to bother you." I said. "I have a question about the equipment."

He seemed a bit surprised. "Okay, what about it?"

"I just wondered who would have access to the stage and getting a microphone cable."

His eyes widened. "Are you talking about the murder?"

So, he'd heard about the murder weapon.

"Yes. I was wondering who would be able to get a microphone cable." No way to hide what I was doing.

"Are you with the police?" he asked.

"I'm investigating the murder."

That wasn't a lie. However, I hadn't admitted that I didn't work for the police either. I just wanted him to offer up any information he had without questioning my credentials.

"Did you see anyone take a microphone with a long cable?" I pressed.

"Actually, I saw someone take one the other day."

"Really?" I asked excitedly. "What did the person look like?"

"He was tall and had blond hair. It was kind of far away, so I couldn't see well." He continued rolling the cable.

"Would you be able to pick him out of a lineup?"

"I'm not sure," he said with a frown.

If I showed him the photos of the impersonators, maybe he would spot the man he'd seen take the microphone. Getting photos of the men might be tough, but I thought I could pull it off. I had no choice but to try. This was a life-and-death situation.

"What's your name?" I asked.

"Huey Hamlin." He peered around, as if he was second-guessing giving his name.

"If I show you photos of some people, would that be okay with you?"

I had no idea what I would do if he said no. He studied my face. With each passing second, I figured the chance of having him agree lowered.

"Yeah, I guess that would be fine," he said.

"Great, thanks," I said. "I'll be in touch."

I hurried away from the stage, contemplating how I would get pictures of these people. Huey watched me for a couple of seconds, then went back to his work. Maybe it was a strange request, but I was happy with the outcome. So far, my potential leads on finding the killer were few and far between. This was exactly the news I had needed.

Now, how would I get pictures of the men? Their flyer photos, which promoted the fair concerts, showed them as Elvis impersonators, so that wouldn't work because they would be in costume. I needed them without the Elvis getups.

"What's going on, gorgeous?"

I clutched my chest when I realized Donald had popped up beside me. "I'll never get used to that paranormal, pop-up-out-of-nowhere thing," I said.

"I suppose I tend to forget that you don't know I'm there."

"How long have you been here?" I asked.

"I was standing with you when you asked the man if he recognized the person and if he would view photos."

"I didn't even realize."

"What's the plan?" he asked. "You just have to find photos of these men?"

"Yes, but that won't be so easy," I said. "I can't just walk up to them and snap a photo."

"Well, you could do some spying and maybe surreptitiously get a photo, like a good private eye."

I raised an eyebrow. "I suppose that would be a good plan. I think I'll give it a try."

"What would you do without me?" Donald said.

"Ha," I said, still pondering about the photos. "I need to find out where these people are so I can track them down. I checked Facebook. Justin's profile is set to private, and the only photo I can see is of his car."

Donald had no suggestion about that.

"I can't do anything tonight, though," I said.

"I'm sure you'll figure out a way. I have complete confidence in you," Donald said.

"Do you really?" I asked.

"Absolutely." He smiled. "I knew when I popped into your trailer that you were a woman who had things under control and knew the right things to do."

"Thanks for the vote of confidence," I said.

His words had been a boost to my ego. Donald and I walked across the midway. Some people moved right through him. They had no idea they were in the path of a ghost. What they didn't know wouldn't hurt them, I supposed.

A short time later, I had moved forward with my plan. Excited shrieks and screams surrounded me. The scent of hot dogs drifted through the air. I peeked around the edge of the Ferris wheel. Justin was right there, standing by the ticket stand. The only problem was, another man stood in front of him, making getting a photo of him impossible. Too bad I didn't have access to the lineup photos. I knew neither Pierce nor Caleb would give them to me.

"Get out of the way," I hissed.

"I don't think they're going to hear you," Donald said.

"No, I guess not," I said.

"Maybe I can do something to help," Donald said.

"Like what?" I asked.

"I can cause a distraction and then maybe they would move." Donald's voice was full of hope.

"Yes, but maybe they'll all walk away at that point," I said.

"It wouldn't be anything drastic, just enough for the person in the way to move. I'll touch him and freak him out."

"Well, if you think it'll work," I said, "that would be helpful."

"I'll give it my best shot," Donald said.

I watched as he ambled over to the men. He gave me a thumbs-up. I just hoped they didn't see me staring at them. They'd for sure get suspicious. Donald stood beside the guy I wanted out of my way. He reached up and tickled the man's nape. The man whipped around as he touched his neck. He'd definitely felt Donald's touch. He probably thought it was a mosquito or something.

Nevertheless, he still hadn't moved out of the way. I motioned again. Donald signaled "okay." The man moved, but so did my target. Why were they moving so much? The men seemed a bit anxious. Donald frowned and I shrugged. I wasn't sure this plan would work out after all.

Donald reached out and touched the guy again. Thank goodness only he moved this time, and I quickly snapped a photo of Justin. I'd zoomed in enough so that with any luck I'd get a good picture of his face.

On to the next subject. I hoped getting a picture of him would be just as easy. Well, not that this one had been a complete cinch, but not too bad, considering it could have been a lot worse.

After snapping another couple pictures, I checked my phone's screen to make sure the images would be adequate. The one of Justin was blurry. How had I let this happen? Now he was gone. How would I find him again?

"I have to find Justin again, Donald," I said. "Unfortunately, his was blurry."

"I'm not surprised that he's not photogenic," Donald quipped.

The night sky dazzled above us with millions of sparkling stars. Those stars would fade the closer I made it to the midway area, where the lights of the rides canceled out the majestic universe above. A warm breeze floated across my skin. Even though it was a beautiful evening, I reminded myself that I needed to be on high alert at all times. I never knew when I might have to escape an attacker. Heaven forbid something like that would happen.

Before I even reached the area, I spotted Justin Blackburn, Maybe this was my lucky night. The man I assumed had lost his shirt behind my trailer was right there practically posing for the shot. He stood by the stage, talking to a couple of other men. This was similar to the last situation, but at least I had a pretty good, clear shot of him if I could just get close enough. I couldn't take the photo from all the way over here. That would guarantee another blurry photo. There was no way anyone would be able to see his face clearly enough. I had to inch closer, but I had to do it without being noticed. Maybe if I just casually walked by. But he might grow suspicious if I did that.

I wanted to hide so he had no idea that I was sneaking up on him to snap a photo. I headed in the other direction, so I could walk behind the stage and loop back around. But then I'd be snapping the picture from the side and I wouldn't be able to get his full face. This was truly a dilemma. Maybe I could just run up to him and capture a photo. Could I take that chance?

"I need your help again, Donald," I said. He could make another distraction and get the guy to turn around.

I just hoped he didn't catch me when I snapped the photo. What other option did I have? There was no other way to get the picture. This was a lot more dangerous than I had anticipated. Pierce and Caleb's words echoed in my head, saying, "I told you so." But this was no time for me to think about a scolding from them.

I headed around the stage, with Donald following alongside me. It was a long way around to the back, and I worried that the men might leave before I reached the other side.

"Okay, so here's the deal," I said. "I need you to be a distraction again."

"I'm game," he said.

"I just want to get him to turn around so I can get a clear picture of him."

"Taking the photo might capture his attention," Donald said.

"That's just the chance I'll have to take, I guess. I need to get these images fast so we can identify the killer."

"I would like that very much," Donald said. "Have I told you how much I appreciate all the work you're doing on this?"

"Think nothing of it," I said. "It's just what I do."

"Much to the chagrin of Pierce and Caleb," he said.

"Yes, they're not happy about it, but I'm not going to let that stop me."

"I think they know that too," he said.

At the edge of the stage, I peeked around the side. The men were still standing in the same spot and talking.

"Okay, here's the plan," I said. "Just like before, go up to him, touch him, and get him to turn around so I can snap a photo."

"Just be careful, standing here alone," Donald said.

"I promise I will."

I watched as Donald walked around the side of the stage and over to the men. They were still talking and had no idea that a ghost was right there behind them. Donald reached out and touched Justin's neck. Justin whipped around to see who was behind him. Of course, no one was there—no one he could see anyway. This was my chance. I held up the phone and snapped a photo. Unfortunately, there was a big flash when this happened, and Justin looked my way. Uh-oh. Just as Donald had warned me.

"Hey, what are you doing?" Justin called out.

This was when I needed to run. Why wasn't I running? Finally, I turned around and dashed down the side of the stage, headed for the back area. If Justin came after me, he'd quickly find me. I needed to find a place to hide. I hoped he hadn't seen my face.

I scanned the surroundings. Just my luck, there were no good hiding spots. My choices were either one of the few trailers around or, of course, under the stage. That might work. Yes, I decided, the best spot was probably under the stage. Maybe I could crawl out on the other side and then get back to my trailer safely.

Getting on my hands and knees, I crawled under the stage. Donald moved under there with me, even though he was invisible to most people. At least he was being a true friend and coming with me. I tensed as I waited for the men to run past. I saw their legs and overheard them talking.

"Where did she go?" one of them asked in a rough voice as they moved by.

Thank goodness they didn't check under the stage.

"You think they're gone?" Donald asked.

I remained quiet. It was too soon for me to speak. I didn't want them to hear me, although the noise from the activity around us meant they probably wouldn't. Too bad Donald couldn't just read my thoughts. How long would I have to stay under here? Would they come back for me or had they gone for good? It certainly had been a close call. I should have known something like that would happen.

A couple more minutes passed with no sign of the men.

"Do you think it's safe to get out of here?" I asked.

"I think they're gone."

I crawled out from under the stage, checking to the left and right. No sign of the men.

"Is it just me or does it seem even darker and scarier now?" I asked.

I needed to get back to the trailer. My mission of collecting photos would have to continue tomorrow.

"I'll keep my eye out for them," Donald said

"Thank you," I said. "The men could come back at any time. It's dark and I can't see anything."

"That's true, Celeste. This is dangerous. Maybe we should have waited until the morning."

When I reached the edge of the stage, I paused again. I

wanted to peek around to make sure the men weren't standing right there. I eased around and, thank goodness, saw no sign of them.

"I think the coast is clear," Donald said. "Don't worry, Celeste, I'll always be here for you."

"Let's get out of here," I motioned.

CHAPTER 28

Travel Trailer Tip #28
Neighbors aren't always friendly. Sometimes you have to watch out for the other campers.

Later in the evening, I was back at my trailer. Pierce had been delayed in coming to see the painting. I supposed he thought it couldn't possibly be the painting he was looking for. I was almost positive, though. I wished he'd hurry up because I didn't like having the thing in my possession.

I'd just put away the paintings from a long day. A steady flow of customers had come through today and I'd sold six paintings. Needless to say, I was ecstatic with that number. I'd even sold the painting of Van as he stared up at the limitless blue sky, with the fairgrounds as the background. Oddly enough, I'd painted that months ago, before I'd even known I'd be here for a craft fair.

Van barked, letting me know that someone was approaching the area. When I glanced over my shoulder, I'd expected to see a customer, but it was the man I'd bought the painting from who was headed my way. Not that he couldn't be a customer, but it was unlikely. Maybe he was just coming to check out my work, as I'd done his. Would he be so enamored with one of my paintings that he would have to have one as I had with one of his?

"How may I help you?" I asked. I'd already packed up my paintings, so I had nothing out to show him. Maybe if he came back some other time. And there were other fairs taking place soon.

"How are you this evening? You remember me, correct?" he asked.

"Of course. I bought that lovely painting from you."

"Well, that's what I wanted to speak with you about," he said.

"What about it?" I asked.

"I'm afraid I need that painting back."

I hadn't expected that.

"Is there a problem?" I asked, trying to act as if I didn't know there was something special about the painting.

"Yes, actually, there is a problem. See, I shouldn't have sold the painting. I forgot that my mother wanted it and she's just been heartbroken ever since."

"Oh, that is terrible," I said.

He wasn't a good liar. The images in my painting had told me to buy his artwork. And he was telling me that I had to give it back? Pierce needed to know about this right away.

If I told him that painting wasn't here and I'd have to go get it, that would give me more time to get in touch with Pierce. Yes, that seemed like my only plan. Pierce would arrest him for stealing the priceless art.

"I don't have it here with me. I'll have to go get it."

A frown slipped across his face. "Could you do that straightaway?"

I didn't believe him. I mean, if his mother wanted it back that badly, surely morning would be fine. It wasn't like this was a painting emergency or anything.

"I'm sorry, I can't do that. I'd be glad to get it for you in the morning."

He glared at me. I knew he was angry.

"I'm afraid that just won't work for me," he said. "It must be this very second. You do understand, don't you?" It seemed more like a threat than a question.

To my surprise, he walked right around me and headed toward my trailer, as if he was going to walk inside.

"I know you have the painting. I saw you put it in there," he snapped.

Had he been spying on me? I'd put the painting in there the day I bought it. It was creepy to know that he had been watching me. Maybe he was just saying that. Yes, that had to be it, but I was still panicking.

"You can't go in there," I said as I ran past him.

I stood in front of the door, blocking him. I assumed he would stop when I stepped in front of him, but I'd been wrong. Instead, he grabbed me, wrapping his hands around my neck, and squeezed tightly. I clawed at his arms, trying to get him to release his hold on me, but nothing worked. Things grew darker by the second. I couldn't let myself panic or he would surely kill me.

I had to think of a way to get out of this. When I tried to scream, nothing came out. To my left, I spotted the easel propped against the trailer. I moved toward it, but I only made it a couple of steps. We tumbled to the ground. With the man on top of me, I was losing hope of ever escaping.

Somehow, I moved my knee upward and jammed him as hard as I could. He tumbled to his left, falling to the ground with a groan. As soon as he was off me, I jumped to my feet. I grabbed the easel and smashed it over his head. In an instant, he was out cold.

I ran away from the trailer. I had to find Caleb. Unfortunately, I knew my phone wouldn't work around here. I should have insisted on a different location when I first realized the phone service was so bad here. It was times like this that I needed that phone desperately.

I ran through the dark night. Panting harder, I sensed someone behind me. He'd probably gotten up from the ground and would be even more furious. I glanced over my shoulder. He wasn't chasing me. Someone *else* was chasing me. My legs just wouldn't move any faster. This was as fast as I could go.

"Stop," the man called out.

His tone didn't sound menacing. Who was this person? Maybe he was trying to help me? I slowed down just a bit and soon he reached me. I recognized him. He wasn't in his Elvis costume this time.

"Are you all right?" Justin asked.

I tried to catch my breath so I could speak. All this time, I'd thought he was the bad guy. *Was* he the bad guy? He was being nice now, so maybe I had misjudged him.

Finally, I said, "I think I'm all right. That man attacked me. I think he must be the killer."

"What man?" Justin asked, peering over his shoulder.

"He's back at my trailer. I need to contact the police right away. But my phone isn't working. It's like being isolated, cut off from the world out here."

"Yes, it is like being cut off from the world, but don't worry, you're with me," Justin said.

It was hard not to worry until I was completely out of danger. I had no idea where my attacker was.

"Do you have a phone with you?" I asked. "Perhaps it works and I can call the police."

"No, I'm sorry. I don't have a phone with me," Justin said.

"Well, in that case, I need to keep running toward the midway. I think my phone will work there. That's where I called the police from before, when I discovered Donald's body."

"Yes, you did discover him, didn't you?" he said with a tinge of something in his voice.

I surveyed the surroundings for the attacker, but I caught no movement. He could be hiding anywhere, behind any of the tall trees or dark trailers. Everyone else was sleeping. I felt as if I was the only one awake out here, except for this man standing with me. Ultimately, he was a stranger too.

The expression on his face gave me pause. Justin stared at me strangely, anger firing in his eyes. Even though he'd offered to help, I decided it was time for me to get out of there.

After pivoting, I walked at a brisk pace. Not too fast, because I didn't want Justin to know I was kind of afraid of him. After a couple more steps in the direction of the midway, my trip was abruptly cut off when he grabbed me from behind. I screamed out, but he covered my mouth with one hand while still holding me around the chest with his other arm.

Chapter 29

Travel Trailer Tip #29
It's okay to ask for help with your travel trailer adventures. Every Sherlock needed a Watson.

Would anyone notice me in the dark, struggling to break free? I moved my arms, kicked my legs, lunged forward, but his grip was just too tight. It seemed as if I was doomed. Justin was dragging me away from the fairgrounds and toward the trees. Once he got me there, I knew it would be all over for me. He would kill me just like he'd killed Donald.

Then—I heard a rustling. The next thing I knew, someone was beside us. The person punched Justin square in the jaw. With the hit, he tumbled backward, and I managed to scramble to my feet. When I saw that it was my dad, I ran to him. He wrapped his arms around me. He wasn't alone either. Sammie and Dallas ran up to us.

"Are you all right?" Papa asked.

"I am now," I mumbled into his chest. "You saved me, Papa."

"That's what fathers are for, sweetheart," he said.

Papa had always been there for me and this time was no different. He'd saved me from the killer. Justin remained on the ground, knocked out cold. He never saw what hit him. My dad was one tough guy. Dallas raced over and restrained Justin's arms just in case he woke before the police arrived. Sammie wrapped her arms around me. The familiar strawberry scent of her shampoo added a layer of comfort to the situation.

"What are you all doing here?" I asked, still somewhat breathless.

"Call it a hunch, I guess. I started thinking about the fun-house thing and it freaked me out. Dallas and I got your dad and came to find you."

Dallas flashed that lopsided grin Sammie liked so much. Maybe I had misjudged the guy.

"Thank you, Dallas," I said. "I appreciate you helping me."

"You're welcome. Anything for Sammie." He practically had hearts in his eyes when he spoke her name.

"That was quite a scene," Donald said. "Like something right out of the movies."

Of course, my father, Sammie, and Dallas had no idea the ghost was here, much less that he'd paid him a compliment. Papa was a pretty modest guy anyway.

"What do we do?" I asked. "We have to get the police over here so they can handcuff this guy. I don't want him getting up and trying to attack me again."

"I won't let that happen," Papa said. "Go ahead and call the police."

"My phone doesn't work here. If we go away to an area where it'll work, he might wake up and get away."

"I've got him under control," Dallas said.

"Dallas and I will stay here with him," Papa said. "You go place the call."

"I don't want you staying here with that killer." I pulled out my phone and checked, just out of curiosity. By some miracle, the phone worked this time. I couldn't believe I had service. I dialed Caleb's number, and thank goodness he answered right away. Would Pierce be upset that I hadn't called him? In my defense, Caleb's number had been the last one called, and therefore easier to dial.

"We have the killer. He's out cold. You have to come quick and handcuff him before he wakes up," I said.

"Celeste? Where are you?" Caleb asked frantically.

"Not too far away from my trailer. I think you'll spot us."

"I'm on my way," he said.

With that, I ended the call. I had to wait. Undoubtedly, minutes would seem like hours.

"Wow, you let him have it," Donald said as he punched the air. "I can't believe you all. Celeste knocked out the guy at her trailer and Eddie knocked out this one. Dallas has the guy pinned down. You guys are a force to be reckoned with."

With all the current action, I'd forgotten all about the guy back at my trailer. He'd wanted that painting so badly. I knew that was because it was way more valuable than the money I'd given him for it. Maybe he'd figured that out too.

Caleb called out my name. I scanned across the way and saw him running toward us. In the distance, sirens sounded and police lights flashed as they pulled up. Thank goodness everyone had arrived. Caleb ran up to the guy and pulled him to his feet, slapping handcuffs on him.

"I hope you have another set of those handcuffs," I said. "Because I forgot about the guy I knocked out at my trailer."

Caleb motioned for an officer to go to the trailer. "You're lucky you got out of this alive."

"I'm assuming he's still there. It's the man I bought the painting from. I've recovered Pierce's stolen painting," I said.

"We haven't confirmed that yet," Pierce said.

I spun around and realized he had approached as well.

"I'm confident I have the stolen painting." I pushed my shoulders back proudly.

"You have that thing secure, right?" Pierce asked.

"Oh please, you're not dealing with a novice," I said. "I told you to hurry up and get over here to look at it."

"How did this happen anyway?" Pierce asked. "You didn't explain much over the phone."

"That's Celeste, always being mysterious," Sammie said.

"Well, Van accidentally spilled solvent on the canvas, and that was when the other picture appeared underneath the one I bought."

"Is the painting all right?" Pierce asked.

"Yes, sure, it's fine," I said with a dismissive wave. "Some minor damage maybe, but it can be restored." I acted as if I dealt with priceless artwork all the time. I knew paint, though, and this time I spoke with confidence that the painting would be just fine.

"If you're sure," Pierce said hesitantly.

"I'm positive. There are no problems with it. Luckily, the artist who painted on top of the original art only wanted to cover it for a short time to disguise it. The paint he used didn't stick, so the priceless painting went mostly unharmed."

An officer led Justin away in handcuffs. He flashed an angry glare at me and then my father, Sammie, and Dallas. I smirked. Maybe I shouldn't taunt the killer. I was much braver when the guy was in handcuffs, that was for sure.

"Celeste, I need to get that painting right away," Pierce said.

"Of course," I said. "Follow me back to the trailer and I'll get it for you."

Pierce walked with me toward the trailer. My father came along too. I figured he was still a bit antsy about what had happened. He didn't want to let me out of his sight, which was understandable. Of course, that made me feel loved. I hated that I had worried him like that, although it was nice to know he was always there for me.

When we made it to my trailer, I opened the door. Van danced around as if he knew something was out of the normal.

"It's right over here," I said.

Pulling out the painting, I showed it to Pierce. He eyed the canvas up and down, studying the artwork. Under the remnants of what I had taken off was the gorgeous piece of art. The impressionistic oil painting depicted a combination of red and pink roses on a turquoise green background. I marveled at the lovely portrayal of nature that had been carried out with large strokes on the canvas. The acrylic rendering of a blackbird perched on a dead oak tree had obviously been carried out in an attempt to conceal the remarkable piece, which was far more stunning.

"That's it, all right. I can't believe you found it." Pierce reached out and hugged me.

I glanced over and noticed that Caleb stood outside the door. It was too late to explain what he saw. Besides, Pierce was only giving me a congratulatory hug. What was I doing with these guys? My emotions were all over the place.

"I have great news for you," Pierce said. "I was telling the art director of the museum in Nashville where the stolen painting was displayed about you, and I showed him some of your work. I have pictures that I've snapped on different occasions on my phone. He would love for you to do a show at his museum."

"Are you serious?" I asked excitedly.

"Completely serious. I think it would be great for you," Pierce said.

"That's amazing."

I couldn't believe Pierce had shown the man my work. Caleb stood in the background as he listened to our exchange. Maybe the museum would want to showcase Caleb's sculptures too. I felt bad that he wouldn't be showing off his work.

"I had no idea that you even had pictures of my work on your phone," I said.

Pierce shrugged. "What can I say? I think I might be your biggest fan."

My dad coughed and then mumbled something.

"He says he's my biggest fan," I said.

Pierce smiled. "Of course. I'll be your second biggest fan."

Caleb coughed too. I didn't know what to say to that. "Let's just say I have a lot of fans." I laughed.

"I should tell him yes to the art show?" Pierce asked. "I'll give him your information?"

"That would be fantastic," I said.

Caleb turned away from the door. He acted as if he was a bit disappointed, but I wasn't sure why. Surely he wanted me to succeed with my artwork. Maybe it was disappointment that he hadn't been the one to get me the show.

"I've been outdone by Celeste again," Pierce said.

My dad wrapped his arms around my shoulders. "That's my girl. If you want a crime solved, just get Celeste Cabot on the case."

"What I need to find out is how the painting ended up here at the fair," Pierce said.

"I think I know the answer to that. I recognized the attempt at painting over the stolen art," I said.

"Really?" Pierce's voice rose with interest.

"Justin was the artist. He brought the painting here to the fair. He stashed it in that man's booth without his knowledge."

"But the vendor sold it even though he knew it wasn't his? Why would he do that?" Pierce asked.

"A sale is a sale, I suppose," I said.

"How did the vendor figure out that there was another painting underneath?" Caleb asked.

"Justin came back looking for the painting. He figured he'd better get it back. His life probably depended on it."

Pierce nodded. "That makes sense."

"It does make sense. It's all coming back to me now," Donald said.

"What's coming back to you?" I asked. "The murder?"

"Yes. Justin was at the last fair. We shared a dressing room. I walked in when he was painting over the art. He explained that he needed a ride to Atlanta because his car had broken down. He'd sold the artwork. He wanted me to take him, but I told him that I couldn't. Of course, that made him angry."

"Angry enough to kill you?" I asked.

"He'd already told me the story of what he was doing. I told him that he needed to do the right thing and return the painting. We had an argument, and that was when I ended up with the cable around my neck and a doughnut in my hand."

How had I gotten involved in the middle of the heist of a priceless piece of art? However it happened, I'd somehow located the art. I supposed it was my psychic sense that made all this happen.

A bright light appeared within the tree line. I shielded my eyes so I could see exactly where it came from, but it was too bright to watch for long. A sense of serenity and peace fell over the entire area.

"I think that light's for me," Donald said with a gesture over his shoulder.

The paranormal beacon grew brighter. "Yes, I suppose it is."

"Oh, before I go, I think you should get doughnuts for everyone," he said. "As a celebration for finding my killer. It's my way of saying goodbye."

"Doughnuts for everyone," I said with a smile. "It's a deal."

"Thank you for everything, Celeste," he said.

"You're welcome." I reached out for a hug, then remembered he couldn't embrace me.

"You were right, it wasn't a car accident that killed me. I'm glad it's all settled." Donald walked away without another word.

Just as he started to head toward the light, he began singing "It's Now or Never." I supposed that was fitting because he couldn't stay any longer. Van barked, as if saying goodbye as well. We watched Donald as he got closer and closer. The closer he grew to the bright light, the more transparent he became, until, finally, he just disappeared. Then poof, the light was gone, as if it had never been there at all.

"I wouldn't believe it if I hadn't seen it," Caleb said.

"Me either," Pierce said.

They would have been amazed if they'd seen him. Having Pierce and Caleb see Donald disappear into the light excited me. They'd seen the magic of the light, and I liked not being the only one to witness it.

"Did you say something about doughnuts?" my dad asked.

I laughed. "Yes, the ghost wants me to buy everyone doughnuts. It's to celebrate that I found his killer."

"Well, if the ghost wants you to buy doughnuts . . . I mean, it is his final wish, am I right?" Papa said.

"All right, but just don't tell Mom. And only one," I said.

"I promise, just one," he mumbled.

My mother wouldn't be happy with me about this, but I had a hard time telling him no. Those big, sad eyes got me every time. I wanted to give him the world. And I knew he felt the same way about me.

"Come on, Papa." I took him by the arm. "Let's go get those doughnuts. How about the bakery around the corner? It's open twenty-four hours."

"Don't be surprised if they know me by name in there," Papa mumbled.

"Sounds good to me," Pierce said as he walked beside us.

"I'm buying," Caleb said as he fell into step with us.

Caleb and Pierce were at it again. It was always the same with them, competing with each other. I wasn't sure that would ever end. I supposed it was a bit endearing sometimes, just not all the time. Justin had been the one to attack me earlier too. Plus, he'd grabbed Madame Gerard, thinking it was me. The police located Kaye in the parking lot and brought her in as an accessory to the crimes. Turned out, Dallas wasn't involved in the killing, but was he a good match for Sammie? What was in store for me now? On to the next craft fair.

Aunt Patsy's Mini Key Lime Pies

1½ cups graham crackers
10 tablespoons unsalted butter (melted, 142g)
⅔ cup granulated sugar
2 large eggs
5 tablespoons Key lime juice (6–7 Key limes)
1 Key lime (zest of)

Crust:

Preheat oven to 350F and line a standard 12-cupcake tin with paper liners.

In a medium bowl, combine graham cracker crumbs, ⅓ cup sugar, and 57g melted butter.

Divide crust evenly among the 12 liners, approx. 1 heaping tablespoon in each. Press firmly into the bottom of each liner.

Bake for 5–7 minutes. Set aside on cooling rack.

Filling:

Preheat oven to 300F.

Prepare a bain-marie (water bath) on the stove.

Once the water is boiling, place eggs, ⅓ cup sugar, Key lime juice, and zest into a large bowl and begin whisking.

Whisk vigorously over the boiling bain-marie until thick and light (approx. 5–10 minutes). Take on and off bain-marie every once in a while to prevent setting/cooking eggs. Alternatively, try using a hand mixer. The mixture is ready when it's light, thick (like pudding), and ribbons form when you run your whisk through it.

Remove from heat and whisk in 85g melted butter.

Pour into pre-baked tart crusts and bake 5–7 minutes

until set. The center of the pies should jiggle just slightly when the pan is nudged.

Cool completely on a wire rack, then place in fridge for at least 2 hours.

Serve cold, topped with whipped cream if desired. Makes 12 servings.

Aunt Patsy's Red Velvet Cinnamon Rolls

15¼ ounces red velvet cake mix (1 box)
2½ cups all-purpose flour, plus more for dusting
2 cups warm water
2½ teaspoons active dry yeast
1 tablespoon vegetable oil
¼ cup unsalted butter, melted (½ stick)
½ cup light brown sugar, packed
1 tablespoon cinnamon
nonstick cooking spray
2 cups cream cheese frosting, warm

In a large bowl, combine the cake mix, flour, water, and yeast.

Pour mixture onto a lightly floured surface and knead until smooth for 5 minutes.

Place dough in a large, oiled bowl, brush the top of the dough lightly with oil, and let rise for an hour in a warm area.

Punch down the dough and roll out on a floured surface to a rectangular shape about 1 centimeter (½ inch) thick.

Brush the melted butter evenly over the dough until covered.

In a small bowl, combine the brown sugar and cinnamon.

Sprinkle the cinnamon sugar evenly over the dough.

Roll up the dough from the bottom to the top.

Cut the dough into 9 even pieces and place them in a 9-inch (23 cm) square baking pan greased with nonstick spray.

Let the dough rise for another hour.

Preheat the oven to 350°F.

Bake the cinnamon rolls for 30 minutes until toothpick comes out clean.

Release the cinnamon rolls from the pan and place on a wire rack set over a baking sheet.

Pour the cream cheese frosting evenly over the top. Serves 9.

Acknowledgments

Thank you to my family and friends. You all have helped me through a lot and for that I am always grateful. A huge thank-you to my agent, Jill Marsal, and my editor, Michaela Hamilton. You're both awesome!

Did you miss the first installment in the Haunted Craft Fair mystery series? No worries!

Keep reading to enjoy an excerpt from *Murder Can Mess Up Your Masterpiece . . .*

Available from Kensington Publishing Corp.

CHAPTER 1

Travel trailer tip 1:
When hooking up a travel trailer, remember to watch out for the hitch.
Your shins will thank you.

With a pitch-black sky full of twinkling stars and a warm summer breeze caressing my skin, I stood in front of my fabulous pink-and-white Shasta trailer. I surveyed the scene as my family helped me prepare for the upcoming festival. Tomorrow was the start of the four-day annual Summer Arts and Craft Fair in my hometown of Gatlinburg, Tennessee. Selling my art was my full-time job now, so I had to make the next few days a success.

The event was being held at the county fairgrounds. Nestled in the middle of a wooded area was an open space that was the perfect location for all kinds of events held year-round, such as the harvest festival in the fall, the Old Timey Christmas Festival, the Spring Tulip Festival, and many other events all summer.

My vendor spot was number forty-one. My adorable little travel trailer would be my home away from home now. I planned on spending a lot of time in it as I traveled the country, bringing my art to each and every state. It would be a fun adventure. At least that was what I reminded myself. I wouldn't be alone in the trailer. My furry companion, a perky white Chihuahua, was always by my side. One of his oversize ears flopped down, and that was how he'd gotten the name Van Gogh.

Currently, my family was on site helping me with my trailer. Mostly they wanted to snoop to see what this new endeavor was all about. My father ran a small engine repair shop right next to my parents' house. He was also a genius at fixing up classic cars—Corvettes, Camaros, GTOs. My mother had the full-time job of keeping my father and brothers out of trouble. Everyone said I looked a lot like my mother, with dark hair and big brown eyes the shade of a scrumptious piece of Godiva chocolate. My two brothers, Stevie and Hank, worked with my father in the shop. The three of them bickered all the time. Oddly, I knew that was their way of showing affection to one another.

Stevie and Hank had been "helping" me since my earliest memory. Like the time they helped repair my tricycle by taking it apart. Every single piece was set out on the front lawn like a jigsaw puzzle. They'd acted as if it was an innocent gesture of kindness. Or when I was in high school and they helped my date for the senior prom by taking him for a ride before the big night. My date was terrified to come anywhere near my house after that. They were my big brothers, though, and I loved them.

"We're going to make this the best-looking booth in the craft fair," my mother said with a wave of her hand.

My father mumbled under his breath as he tried to untangle the string lights that were meant to hang along the front of my trailer. My mother had volunteered my father for the job. It wasn't that he didn't want to help, it was just that he always had the best intentions but something disastrous happened.

"Look, the lights are tiny little campers just like yours." My mother pointed. "I ordered them from Amazon."

"They're great, Mom, but we'd better help Papa before he trips over the lights and kills himself."

I had the rest of the evening to set up for the craft fair. It had seemed like plenty of time at first, but now I was realizing the sun had set quite some time ago and the clock was ticking. I had to make sure I had all my paintings, blank canvases, and paint for when inspiration came, not to mention I needed to make sure I had everything planned for the setup. If customers couldn't see my paintings, they surely wouldn't buy them.

"I love that you got some of your art framed." My mother touched one of the gold frames.

"I thought it was nice to make some available already framed and some without, in case customers want to pick out their own frames."

"That's good thinking. Isn't our daughter smart?" My mother turned her attention back to my father.

My father mumbled something unintelligible again as he attempted to get the lights untangled from around his neck.

"I told you he'd hang himself." I ran over to him. "How did you do that, Papa?"

My mother and I spun my dad around so that the lights would come undone from around his neck.

"Can you breathe okay?" I fanned him.

He waved his hand. "I'm fine. Don't fuss."

My mother rolled her eyes. "He'd say he was fine even if he was blue-faced and passed out on the ground."

"Hey, is this thing supposed to be locked?" Stevie yelled out.

Just then, the back of the trailer tipped, making one side shoot up in the air like a seesaw.

"What have you done?" I shouted.

Hank ran over to help Stevie. "That's not how you do it. Let me show you how it's done."

As Hank raced toward the trailer like a bull charging toward the matador's red cape, he tripped over his own feet and landed face-first in the mud.

"Oh, for Pete's sake," my mother said.

Stevie laughed. "Thanks for the help, bro."

"Let me show you all how it's done." I gestured for everyone to step out of the way.

"Be careful, honey," my mother called out.

The guy who'd sold me the trailer had showed me all about it. Sure, I wasn't an expert, but I couldn't be any worse at this than my brothers.

As I worked on the hitch, my mother yelled at my father, "Be careful on that ladder."

Oh no. He had the ladder. This wouldn't end well.

Would the rest of the evening be spent in the emergency room? Once I secured the hitch, I hurried over to my father's side. I held the ladder as he teetered on the edge of the top rung. The roll of tape slipped from his hands, landing on the ground. As soon as I let go of the ladder to pick up the tape, the ladder swayed and my father tumbled to the ground.

"I knew that would happen," my mother said.

While I helped my father to his feet, Van snatched the roll of tape and darted toward the nearby giant oak tree.

"Van, come back with the tape." I chased after my four-legged companion.

Of course, he thought this was a game and was determined to win. My brothers yelled for Van to stop as they ran behind me. After a couple of minutes of playing chase-the-Chihuahua around the old oak tree, I scooped up Van with the roll of tape still dangling from his mouth.

I handed the tape back to my father. "Are you okay, Papa?"

"I've had worse falls than that," he said.

Unfortunately, that was true.

"Do you think you should climb back on that ladder?" I asked as he walked away.

"There's no talking to him. He won't listen," my mother said.

We watched as my father climbed back onto the ladder with my brothers supervising. Stevie and Hank bickered back and forth about who would hold the ladder.

"I've never seen such chaos," a female voice said from over my shoulder.

I spun around to find my best friend, Sammie, standing behind me. Samantha Sutton, or Sammie as everyone affectionately called her, and I had been friends since first grade. Of course, to be friends for that long we had a lot in common. We both liked eighties music, lounging by the pool in the summer, and bargain shopping. As for appearance, we were complete opposites. Sammie was tall, with long legs, and I was short. She had blond hair cut into a bouncy bob and I had long, dark hair.

"When did you get here?" I asked as I reached out to hug her.

"You mean, how much of this scene did I witness? Enough to see that it's business as usual for the Cabots."

I blew the hair out of my eyes. "Welcome to my world."

"I'm fully aware of your world, remember? It's been this way for the total of all the years I've known you." She handed me a pretty pink package.

She knew how much I loved the color pink. Pretty much everyone knew pink was my signature color when they spotted my old pink truck pulling the pink trailer.

"What is this?"

"A little something I thought might make you feel better."

"You bought me a gift? Why did you do that? You didn't have to do that." I immediately untied the white ribbon.

"I know I didn't have to, but it's just that tomorrow is a big day for you. A whole new start to life." She moved her arm in a sweeping gesture. "It deserves a celebration."

I hugged her again. "Thank you. You're such a great friend."

"Hurry and open it. I want to see if you like it."

I hurriedly opened the package. The suspense was getting to me. My mother had slipped over to see what all the fuss was about.

"Oh, you're ruining the paper," my mother said. "We could reuse that."

My mother wanted to keep every bit of gift wrap she saw. We'd exchanged the same gift bags back and forth for six years now. If one got smashed or ripped she grieved for days.

I eased the pink paper away from the box and handed it to my mother. She slowly folded it, as if it were a piece of delicate silk. I pulled the mug from the box. A self-portrait of Vincent Van Gogh was on each side.

"Do you love it? When you pour in hot liquid his ear disappears."

I laughed. "It's perfect."

"Interesting," my mother said.

The sound of a motor caught our attention. The man in charge of organizing the craft fair was driving a golf cart down the path in front of our booths. With his wide shoulders and hefty stature, Evan Wright barely fit behind the wheel of the vehicle.

"Who's this guy?" Stevie asked with a hint of suspicion in his voice.

"He's the guy in charge here," I whispered.

"He seems shady if you ask me," Hank said.

My brothers, mother, and father were suspicious

of everyone. I tried not to be that way, although I supposed on occasion I succumbed to that attitude too.

Evan rolled to a stop in front of my booth. "It's a bit late to be out, don't you think?"

"There's a curfew?" Sammie asked.

Evan eyed Sammie. "No curfew, but people are trying to sleep because they'll be up early in the morning. I heard a lot of ruckus over here."

"Ruckus," Hank said with a chortle. "That's a funny-sounding word."

Stevie laughed too.

My mother smacked them on the back of the head with the gift wrap remnants. She meant business if she was jeopardizing her paper.

Evan tapped his fingers against the steering wheel while waiting for an answer. The gold ring on his finger clanked against the metal of the wheel.

"We were just wrapping up," I said with a forced smile.

He scrutinized all of us for a bit longer before accelerating away.

"That was weird," Sammie said.

"Well, it takes all kinds," my mother said.

"Ta-da," Papa said.

The string lights glowed in the night sky. They added just the right amount of coziness to the area. It didn't feel quite as lonesome now. I'd worried that I'd get lonely once my family left. Yes, I couldn't believe I'd thought that, but I had.

I hugged my father. "The lights are fantastic. Thank you, Papa."

"Well, I should go and let you get some rest before

your big day tomorrow." Sammie raised her voice, hoping my family would take the hint and leave too.

She'd obviously noticed my yawning. The family didn't catch subtle hints, or if they did, they ignored them. Tomorrow was Friday, the start of the fair. I needed to rest for the big event, but with my excitement, I wasn't sure how I'd ever fall asleep.

My mother surprisingly picked up the clue. "Boys, it's time to go." She clapped her hands.

Somehow my mother rounded up my brothers and father. Sammie left too. I clutched Van in my arms. It was just the two of us. Tomorrow was the big day.